Jacques Bergur

GOEBIUS' STRANGE MODEL

To my family, to my friends…

Thanks to:

Richard Feynman, Douglas Hofstadter, Richard Dawkins, Jean-Claude Ameisen, Isaac Asimov, and the many other enlightened minds who asked good questions, tried to answer them … and were able to share their findings.

… And also to:
Marine who ensured the medical and emotional coherence of this story, and Thomas who ensured its logic and scientific consistency.

… And always to:
Monique, for her patience and guidance during the slow gestation of this book.

… As well as to:
Michel Saint-Germain who was the first to believe in this strange story.

… And to:
Shelley for her patient and careful review and correction of the English release, as well as Monique and Dwight T.M. for their comments.

TO THE HURRIED READER:

Some of the elements of logical reasoning presented in this story require a little attention and effort. The impatient reader can ignore them and accept their conclusions, without it being detrimental to the understanding of the story. However, it would be a pity not to ponder such reasoning because there is payoff down the road...

FOREWORD

When the idea to write this story first arose, I had in mind to write a thriller involving scientific concepts.

However, after scientific and literary professionals read it, it seems that it is rather a suspense novel about science...

But after all, does it really matter?

This story is a parable, a ride between determinism and randomness, where starting from a riddle usually attributed to Henri Poincaré, the benevolent shadows of Newton, Gödel, Turing, Moebius, and others hover...

At the reader's discretion, this journey can be undertaken and understood along three possible routes:

-As a plot with multiple unexpected twists and turns until its conclusion.

-As an unexpected encounter, in plain language and without mathematics, with a few concepts usually restricted to insiders, but which are essential in order to try to understand the world in which we are all immersed. Thus isomorphisms, chaos, entropy, emergence, and strange loops invite themselves discreetly, although in a determinant way, into the fictional landscape and the plot.

-Finally, those who analyze the story's structure will discover that through multiple self-reflections, the structure itself mirrors the concepts evoked.

If, after having read this book, the reader has been entertained, and feels the desire to deepen his or her knowledge on the exciting concepts touched upon in this story, then this book will have achieved its modest objective.

1 - DINNER

"Will you have some salad?" my neighbor was saying. I nodded yes. What else could I do?

Obviously, I could understand what I was told…

There were at least fifty guests sitting in a circle in a huge round vaulted hall made of exposed stones.

All these people were silently eating, exchanging only the few words necessary to maintain decorum during the meal.

But did I actually know how to speak?

It seemed to me that I had never tried.

Had I ever existed before the moment when my neighbor had offered me some salad?

At least I couldn't remember; still it seemed to me that I had a name.

Something like Li-O.

Near the center of the circle was a buffet meal, and a couple of waiters offered dishes so that the guests could help themselves or serve their neighbors. The two waiters were young and athletic; they could have been brother and sister, not so much because of the similarity of their facial features, but rather because of the expression of cold indifference on their faces.

I stealthily looked at the man to my right who had offered me some salad, then looking to the other side, I could see that my left neighbor was a woman. She silently offered me some soda water, and looking further around the room I could see that we were a group of men and women, apparently sitting in no specific order around the outer circle of the table. Something was striking: all these men and women had an air of resemblance. The whole assembly was composed of adults, each with a well-proportioned physical appearance and an almost non-expressive face. Each of them looked absorbed in their own meditation. Did I look like them…?

The plates, mugs, and carafes were made of black enameled stoneware, decorated with golden geometrical patterns. The cutlery seemed to be made of frosted silver. All of these created a harmonious whole.

The meal was excellent and would have been rather pleasant if some conviviality had breathed a little animation into the gathering. After the duck breast with red berries and the cheese, just as the neighbor on my left was passing me a slice of cake, with the same indifference and icy politeness that seemed to inhabit all of us, something surprising happened. It lasted only for a fraction of a second. Maybe I looked astonished as her eyes briefly met mine, but she seemed unaffected and looked away. I noticed her empty glass, and I felt that I had to offer her some water, which gave me the opportunity to realize that I could speak.

When the meal was over, a kind of carillon sounded, and I stood up without thinking. Not knowing why, I turned my back to the center of the circle, and at the same time as the others, I moved away from the center towards the circular wall of the hall. I came up against a solid wood door, as the others did. On the door there was a small card on which was written in green ink "Come in". Obviously I could read as well…

As I was stepping through the doorway, I could see that the other guests were also stepping through their doors. Mine gave access to a small corridor a few meters long, leading to a room of about two hundred square feet. A large carpet covered the paving slabs of the floor. The walls were made of exposed stones, identical to those in the hall from which I had come, and a thick curtain seemed to conceal a window. Set in the wall, adjacent to the wall with the window, was a heavy wooden door carved with geometric patterns. There was a large single bed, a massive wooden desk and a solid wooden wardrobe in warm shades, two wooden chairs and a brown leather armchair. A small bathroom was attached to the room. The whole appeared to be undoubtedly comfortable. However, there was no mirror in the bathroom.

At this moment, I realized that I had not seen any objects in the entire place that could reflect an image.

I tried to open the carved wooden door but it was locked. I went to the desk and found a white notepad, several different colored pens, and envelopes. One of the envelopes was sealed and the word 'Open' was written in the same green ink. I sat in the armchair, opened the envelope; inside there was a sheet of paper where the following message was printed in red:

'**First Warning**: *you have looked surprised; this is strictly forbidden.*'

An oppressive feeling came over me.

At the bottom of the page, in smaller letters, was written what appeared to be a quote or a motto.

'Those who, through their efforts, will firmly hold the rope,
Soon shall master their fate, and be able to cope.'

I began to inspect the contents of the wardrobe. It contained clean linen, underwear as well as shirts, trousers, jackets and a pair of shoes. The colors of the clothes were rather austere and sober, just like those the other guests and I were already wearing. Then I opened the top drawer of the desk; there was a notebook with a red cover, entitled:

'The Fundamental Survival Rules'

On the front page, as if by way of introduction, a threatening sentence was written in red letters:

'*The following rules are very serious; obey them, because the danger is immense.*'

Then, on the next page, a kind of children's rhyme was written in calligraphy:

Not to disappear, the following rules shall you always obey:
- Personal feelings shall you never show, and the following rule shall you always obey:
- Personal questions shall you never ask, and the following rule shall you always obey:
-Personal answers shall you never give, and the following rule shall you always obey:

- Personal appearances shall you never mention, and the following rule shall you always obey:
-Silent shall you remain each day unless previously addressed.

The other pages of the notebook were blank except for the motto written in small letters at the bottom of each page:
'Those who, through their efforts, will firmly hold the rope,
Soon shall master their fate, and be able to cope.'
I put the notebook back on the desk, and I went to the curtain. Indeed it concealed a window that I could not open; and beyond the panes, the fog and the night created a total darkness.

I suddenly felt deeply tired, and I took off my clothes; and in doing so I noticed that I was wearing a necklace, fitted closely around my neck, which I was not able to remove.

I fell into a heavy dreamless sleep.

2 - PROJECT

The e-mail clearly stated that Matthew's presence at the meeting was mandatory, and that the subject, although not disclosed, was of utmost importance. While he was lost in speculation about what might motivate such a summons, Alex poked his head around the door.

"You've got two minutes for me?"

"Of course, come in!"

A little older than him, Alex was a man about thirty-five years old, clear-eyed, and with an energetic appearance. Matthew liked to work with him because, in his eyes, he combined skill, energy, and modesty, a mixture of rare qualities in their environment... at least with regard to the last one.

"For once, I'm not coming to discuss work with you," he continued. "Warm weather is approaching and I wanted to know if you have plans for the next long weekend?"

"Nothing planned at the moment," replied Matthew, "but I'm planning to relax for a couple of days to clear my mind."

"Well, I promised a friend to take his sailing boat from Bonifacio and deliver it to Mahon. Kristen was supposed to come with me, but she can't, and I wondered whether you might want to replace her. "Besides," he added, "I know that just like me, you love scuba diving. And if we take an extra day off once we are there, maybe we will have time for one or two dives. I've heard about a beautiful underwater cliff full of magnificent gorgonian corals."

While he appreciated Alex and knew Kristen too, Matthew was not particularly close to the couple, and he felt a little surprised, although pleasantly, by the invitation from his colleague. He thought for a moment. Whether it be on his tiny sailboat or in life, he was somewhat fed up with sailing alone since… Therefore he did not hesitate very long before answering.

"Okay! But this is the only circumstance when I will agree to replace your wife!" He added, laughing. "By the way, what is the size of the boat?"

"35 feet. Will it be all right?"

"Perfect!"

"Well, we're both under pressure, as usual; we can talk after the meeting. I assume that you don't know more than I do regarding what all this is about." Alex's assumption was correct.

Once again, Matthew was going to be late. Whatever his reasons might be, he knew for sure that some of his colleagues would not miss an easy opportunity for a sarcastic remark. He rushed through the corridor, and on reaching the closed meeting room door, he ran into Plantin, the Head of the Legal Service.

Unlike him, Plantin was almost never late. Amused, and with a hint of joy, which he qualified in his mind as 'preventive revenge', Matthew thought that their simultaneous arrival would cut short any attempt of snide remarks. 'So much the better', Sarcastic Rudy who was a formidable expert in the art of nasty remarks combining both a sense of humor and political savvy, would not have the opportunity to exercise his talents to Matthew's detriment.

When they entered the room, Rudy laughed and blurted out, "Only five minutes late; for one of them, for once this is an improvement! But the other, probably under his influence, is moving in the wrong direction."

"This meets the average; everything is fine," retorted Matthew.

While Plantin was quietly sitting, the Boss had a faint smile on his lips. He was silently observing this exchange. The Boss was a man in his mid-fifties, who probably was used to some self-discipline, because in spite of his tired face, he had kept a supple and firm physique. After conducting a review of the current projects and of the immediate commercial prospects, the meeting took a more serious tone.

The situation was serious and could be summed up in four alarming findings:

- For the last two years the company had not produced any major innovations.

- The last major contracts had been won over by our competitors.

- The portfolio of current projects was running out as they were almost completed.

- Analysts were beginning to realize this, and the company stock price was falling.

The Boss concluded:

"If we do not get back on the right track within the next eighteen months, we will have to reduce our staff costs, and if our shares continue to fall, we could soon fall prey to a hostile takeover. It is obvious that if this happens, the fate of the company will no longer be in our control. And we will have little say on the potential reorganization."

'*To reduce staff costs, nice understatement...*' thought Matthew.

When the meeting ended, the Boss asked Matthew to come to his office.

The blue-grey, slightly narrowed eyes of the Boss looked into those of Matthew. When he focused on his interlocutors, he looked like a cat gauging a new encounter.

"In your opinion, how can we rectify the situation?" He asked point blank.

'*Vast subject... He must not have waited for me to think about it,*' Matthew thought.

"Everyone knows that innovation is not decided overnight;" he mused aloud, "rather it is the result of a long investment policy, work of a research and development department, and also, of course, hint of gut-feeling and luck that make a company choose the right direction. It is true that the last couple of years, whenever we were close to proposing something really innovative, we were outdone by competitors right before the final finish line."

"Of course we can blame bad luck," said the Boss, "but that won't move us forward, and besides, is this recurrent bad luck really a coincidence?"

As Matthew nodded the Boss added, "Sometimes you have to pave new ways and use lateral thinking methods to obtain unexpected and innovative results."

'*I'm about to find out what he's getting at,*' thought Matthew

Then the Boss explained his project to Matthew.

Or rather 'The Project'

An incredible project.

A project such that Matthew would have never dared to imagine it.

He came out of his meeting with the Boss totally stunned.

When he had asked when all this would start, the Boss had replied "Immediately", and when Matthew had asked who would create the teams and manage the project, he had simply said "You".

The Boss had even given the project a code name: 'Project SUCH'. Then he had added that, in order to prevent accidental or harmful leaks to competitors, the project was to remain secret as long as possible.

Thus it was up to Matthew to find a "blanket project" and make up the different teams which would work best towards the final goal. Each team would remain unaware of the existence of others. It was clear that as the work progressed, it would become necessary to make more and more team members aware of its real purpose. Matthew had carte blanche to decide when and who would be allowed to know what.

As he was about to leave the room, the Boss had added:

"I don't want to put more pressure on you, but this project is our last card, and it rests on you."

'*It's fortunate that he doesn't want to put pressure on me...*' Matthew mused.

"By the way, I know that you will be away for a few days."

"Indeed," Matthew had answered, "I promised Alex to sail his friend's boat from Bonifacio, Corsica, to Mahon in the Balearic Islands; but I can try to arrange otherwise."

"No, no, don't change your plans. A few days of reflections at sea will certainly be useful to get you into a 'lateral thinking' mode."

Then he had added with a smile:

"Try not to drown; we cannot afford to lose our best project manager and our chief engineer!"

That night, reflecting on his day, a detail left Matthew puzzled: between their discussion and the meeting, Alex had not had the time to talk to the Boss about their future absence; hence, he probably had announced their joint absences before even talking to Matthew. "Modest but confident in his intuitions..." he thought.

3 - REFLECTIONS

When I woke up, my first instinct was to look out the window. The day had dawned, but the thick fog made it possible only to distinguish a courtyard and some massive trees whose silhouettes were hardly perceptible. I took a shower. I was able to shave, despite the absence of mirrors, thanks to the electric shaver I found in the bathroom; and the skin of my face was now smooth under my fingers. Then I went to the hall where I had dined the night before.

A few people were already wandering around a buffet on which a large breakfast was arranged. The room was gradually filling up, and people seemed to sit around small tables at their own discretion.

Spotting 'my neighbor of the night before', I went over to her, determined to strike up a conversation and to obtain some answers to the multitude of questions jostling in my head.

While I was approaching her table, the previous warnings found in my room, as well as the first and last strange 'Survival Rules' came back to my mind:

-Personal feelings you shall never show...
-Silent shall you remain each day unless previously addressed.

And so I found myself sitting in front of her without daring to open my mouth. She looked at me with the same polite indifference as on the eve, and greeted me with a nod. An oppressive uneasiness came over me. Thus it was impossible to have an explanation about what I was living; it was not even possible to speak...

Just then, passing by our table without stopping, the man who had been my neighbor to the right during the dinner looked at the young woman and murmured "Hello" to her. She returned his greeting; as if it was a signal for her, she turned her beautiful impassive face to me. And looking at the two croissants and the cup of coffee I had brought, she told me with a neutral voice that there were cakes, pancakes, as well as fruit juices at the other end of the buffet. I felt like thanking her warmly, not so much for the information that she had given me, but for having broken the oppressive silence. However, according to the 'survival rule' number one, I refrained and just murmured a polite "Thank you," keeping my face and look as indifferent as possible.

The hall which at first had been silent was now filling with brief murmurs interrupting long periods of silence. We were no exception and everyone was absorbed in their own thoughts. Strangely mine were no longer completely directed towards existential questions, but they were much more prosaic:

'*She keeps an impassive face and does not ask any question; this is the attitude she should have if she were submitted to the same rule as I am. She spoke first, but after she was spoken to, and the last rule seems to also apply to her.*'

Such were my thoughts when, looking at her, I saw the same strange phenomenon as the day before. But it lasted much longer than a flash and persisted for several seconds. According to the warning I had read, I was not allowed to look surprised; hence I did not show any astonishment.

I left her and went back to my room. I grabbed some paper and a pencil, and I walked back through the hall to what seemed to be the exit. The fog had dissipated under a generous sun, and I could see a large courtyard and some tall trees with slightly yellowing leaves inviting me for a visit. Along each side of the courtyard, regularly spaced benches were placed. The temperature was pleasant, if a little chilly, and I sat on an empty bench to think. The courtyard had gradually filled with men and women that I had seen in the hall, some walking, others sitting on the benches, and all of them seemed lost in deep thoughts.

I was almost certain that the woman I called now 'my left neighbor' was subjected to the same constraints as I was. What about the others?

Thinking about it from an external point of view, we probably all appeared to have the same attitude, and that would be the case if we were all subjected to the same rules. However, if my neighbor had talked to me, it was because someone had spoken to her before. And in such a case the person who had talked to her had heard another person talking to him.

Thus 'someone' was different and must have been the first one to talk this morning. To sum up my reflections, I wrote: '*They might all be just like me (except one of them, at least)*'

I began to walk in the courtyard. While I was looking at the others walking, to my amazement, several times and for several seconds, I noticed the same strange phenomenon on some of them that I had already observed twice with my neighbor. And the ominous warning 'Do not look surprised,' always came to mind.

I was deeply surprised not only by the situation I was in, but also by myself. Indeed, my thoughts were mostly engaged in deciphering where I was, and in studying the behavior of the members of the small community I was a part of. But paradoxically, I had to concentrate in order to think about the deeper questions that normally I should have had been worrying about. Why did I care about this phenomenon which I considered amazing, I who had no earlier memories than the dinner of the night before?

The following lunch and dinner took place in the same atmosphere of cold and polite indifference as the previous meals. Back in my room, I found a note on my desk written in green ink and saying: *'It is quite fortunate for you that you have taken the warning into account and that you have applied the survival rules.'*

I fell into a deep sleep again.

4 - CONVICTIONS

Under normal circumstances, Matthew was driven by a boundless curiosity. He conceived his life as a mountain to be climbed and explored, while exercising his free will in choosing the most beautiful route and the most elegant way to accomplish it. This attitude gave him an open nature. He was accustomed to effort, but also open to the sense of danger and the concept of calculated risk. Hence he was aware of the extraordinary aspect of the project entrusted to him, and this ignited his curiosity. Yet, he was also aware of the scale of his responsibility which extended far beyond himself, his company, and his co-workers…

Puzzled, he did not know how to manage all this. During his previous night's watch, he had been mulling over the problem. Upon his return to the office, he would have to define the tasks, establish the teams, delineate and allocate objectives, while ensuring that none of the project members had all the necessary elements to discover its finality.

At first, all this seemed impossible. Indeed how could one envision having several teams working together towards a common objective without them knowing the final goal?

It was becoming clear to him that there would not be just one but several 'cover projects', and each of these projects would have to be an element of the final objective.

The weather was gray, and the boat pitched in a long swell out of nowhere. There was not enough wind to activate the wind vane steering, and once again the autopilot was not working. Alex was asleep in the forward cabin. The sails, not knowing on which breeze to lean to come back to life, moved in all directions. They tossed from one side of the boat to the other. The land had disappeared behind the horizon, two sailing days away.

Matthew took the helm, and let his eyes wander over the circular horizon that surrounded him. '*If I had been less involved in my work and in my passion for the sea, perhaps she would have stayed...*'

Then he looked up at the grey vault, like a roof above his head. '*We are really in a bubble,*' he thought, '*a space bubble, a weather bubble, a time bubble...*'

Interrupting his nostalgic daydream, he took a look at the compass, whose rose was gently swaying behind the steering wheel. They had deviated from their course, and instead of heading westward as expected, the compass indicated that they were heading north-east. '*That's odd*', he thought, '*I held the helm firmly and for sure the course shouldn't have changed.*'

He hauled the jib and mainsail sheets to prevent them from moving and started the engine. He thought that with some speed they would follow a more stable course. Then he went back into his reverie, lulled by the waves and the engine purr.

Moments later, a glance at the compass showed him that they were now heading south. Coming back to reality, he decided to use an experimental method. He focused on the helm and forced himself not to look at the compass for a few minutes. He was deeply convinced that he had not veered off course because he was holding the helm firmly using all his senses to keep on track. After a while he looked at the compass which indicated that they were heading full north. Hence, all this was not due to the sailboat, but to his own feelings and sensations. Although he was convinced that he was staying on course, in the absence of indications from the instrument, indeed he was following a fanciful path.

'*The compass,*' he mused, '*is a little like a rope which guides us in the dark towards our goal... Provided you don't lose your grip... It indicates a heading, independent from the brain. It does not indicate "the right heading" because a heading is neither good nor bad in itself. But the compass allows me to choose my direction, good or bad, with regard to something external.*

Well, I departed from Corsica and I want to go to the Balearic Islands. If I follow my personal conviction, I risk not only missing the final destination, but also sailing around in circles. It seems akin to life... or even akin to the fate of mankind... Strong personal convictions without outside references are not enough to stay the course because they are misleading.'

It was not his first time confronting this apparent paradox of conflicts between personal convictions and reality, and he concluded in his mind, '*Never rely solely on your own personal convictions, as they are often misleading,*' then he immediately added, '*and this is a personal conviction,*' which left him puzzled... But after a while he saw an exit to his "Gödelian" loop: This was not a personal conviction; it was a matter of experience!

The wind which was beginning to gently fill the sails interrupted Matthew's thoughts, and since the boat now had the wind for reference, Matthew activated the wind vane steering. The boat came to life again and resumed its journey towards the creek of Mahon.

5 - INDUCTION

The next morning as we all gathered in the main hall, no doubt remained. The strange phenomenon which I had glimpsed several times was not a hallucination; some people including my 'left neighbor', were subject to it. The top of their heads were now permanently adorned with a kind of yellow halo about ten centimeters in diameter. Despite their solar color, the halos did not seem to cast any radiation, neither heat nor shadow. As a matter of fact, it seemed that it was the color of the air itself that was different above their head and that looked like a halo. I could see that four people were subject to this phenomenon; however nothing in their behavior indicated that they were aware of it. Now I knew by heart the threatening children's rhyme:

Not to disappear, the following rules shall you always obey:
- Personal feelings you shall never show, and the following rule shall you always obey:
- Personal questions you shall never ask, and the following rule shall you always obey:
-Personal answers you shall never give, and the following rule shall you always obey:
- Personal looks you shall never mention, and the following rule shall you always obey:
-Silent shall you remain each day, unless previously addressed.

This time, since no one had spoken to me, I remained silent. In fact it seemed that no one had initiated the domino effect which probably allowed people to speak. A heavy silence reigned in the hall, and only the clattering of the breakfast crockery could be heard.

Suddenly a deep voice filled the room, both calm and impressive:

'Those who cannot see their own halo, will leave before tomorrow night, otherwise they will disappear.'

Complying with the threatening rhyme, no one seemed to react to the announcement. Then the carillon rang and everyone left the hall. Back in my room, I took my notebook and I noted: 'No mirror, no one to talk to, how are they going to know that they must leave this place?' Then I saw the sentence I had written the day before: *'They might all be just like me (except one of them, at least).'*

All just like me… Which ones are like me? Those who have the halo? Or the others? And so, I came to a disturbing conclusion which I had not realized at first. Maybe I was personally affected by this notice to leave under threat of disappearing. There was nothing to let me know whether or not I had a halo. Once again I felt overcome by a strong feeling of oppression.

At lunch, everyone was still there, and I had plenty of time to find out that nothing distinguished the behavior of the four 'enlightened' guests from that of the others. At the end of the meal, a voice sounded again still calm and threatening, but it was not the same voice, and this time it was brief:

'There are still some who have to leave.'

It seemed that since the first announcement there was hardly anyone in the courtyard, and that most of us preferred to retire to our room. As I was wondering for the hundredth time what I had to do, I decided to read again the warnings and the survival rules noted in the book. Just behind the cover I found an envelope, and still the same word written in green: 'Open.' In the envelope, a paper sheet stated:

'All guests in this place reason in the same way.'

And further down: *'There will be as many announcements as necessary.'*

For dinner, I noticed that everyone was there, and that no behavior had changed. My feeling of oppression gave way to a feeling of anguish when, at the end of the meal, before the carillon sounded, a voice was heard for the third time and repeated the message in a shorter way, merely stating:

'Some still remain...'

As the other night, despite my concern, I immediately fell asleep.

The next morning at breakfast, the same scene was repeated, with the same warning at the end of the meal.

'Some still remain...'

At lunch, all the guests were here, nothing had changed, and the eerie message was heard:

'Some still remain...'

The ultimatum was about to expire, and all those who were to leave had to do so before the evening. Anxiously walking up and down my room, I tried with all my strength to know what I had to do. I read and reread the first warning and the rhyme with the rules of survival. I remembered the breakfast when it was said that some of us had to leave the premises under threat of disappearing, and I also remembered the meals when we had been reminded all this, as well as the last message that I had found and which said that all of us reason in the same way.

And early in the afternoon, I had found... It was not an intuition... or a conviction. It was beyond doubt... A certainty... I knew I was one of those who had to leave.

Beyond the relief brought by this discovery, the question was to know how to leave. The vaulted hall was only leading to the courtyard or to my room and I had not seen any way out in the yard. Just to see, I headed to the carved wooden door in my room that I had not been able to open.

To my surprise, I clearly heard a clicking sound that my approach seemed to have activated. And when I pulled the handle, the door opened, giving access to a staircase climbing towards uncertain places.

6 - INTUITIONS

They had reached Port Mahon, and were to leave by plane two days later. So they decided to use the one-day lag to dive on the underwater cliff mentioned by Alex. He had listened to Matthew's philosophico-nautical reflections about convictions in absence of outside references with nodding assent, but had not pursued the discussion.

But while he was installing the regulator on his air tank and checking the pressure, Alex proposed a little game.

"It's a dive '*in the blue*'; the top of the rocky cliff we want to reach is at a depth of 35 meters. Let's go down vertically facing the coast without watching our compass, and let's see whether we are able to still face the cliff when we reach it."

As a matter of fact it was a dive 'in the grey' because there was no sun. However, the water was rather clear. Just before jumping into the sea, Alex had added, "We will have to take care... They say that there is a muddy area at the end of the top the cliff, and of course we have to avoid it."

Matthew had sunk first, head down trying not to change his orientation relative to the shore, that is to say facing the expected cliff. While reaching a depth of 30 meters he saw the cliff taking shape a few meters below, in a direction opposite to what he was expecting; he had turned one hundred and eighty degrees...

As he was rectifying his position in order to rest on the cliff, he looked up and saw Alex also correcting his orientation to also land on the top of the cliff. Unfortunately, perhaps because of a slight current, they had drifted to the muddy area, and when they began to use their fins, both were surrounded by a thick cloud of mud. The light, already reduced at this depth, turned to total darkness. Unable to see Alex, Matthew had to use his fins to move away from the cloud, but this added to the fog of mud. In total weightlessness not only had he lost his orientation, but he was unable to know whether he was swimming upwards or downwards. Although still wrapped in the cloud, he had slightly moved away from the top of the cliff, and the water cleared up somewhat. He could now distinguish the bubbles formed by the air that he was exhaling and so regained lifesaving guidance. Thus he avoided ascending too fast or conversely ending his life at the foot of the cliff, with a narcosis in 65m water depth. When he was able to read his depth gauge again, it exceeded 40 meters.

Alex had carried out the same operation. They gradually went up to 35 m and completed their dive by visiting the rocky part of the top of the cliff, avoiding the dangerous fog of mud.

As Matthew moved his head close to a rock, a part of it took a light grey color; two big eyes appeared and gazed through his mask. He slowly approached his hand but the octopus went away marking its disapproval with a cloud of black ink.

While he was making his decompression stops, he thought about his dive and his encounter with the octopus, this mysterious animal that knows how to simulate the colors and patterns of its surroundings with its skin, camouflaged to such an extent that it can completely disappear into its environment. With a brain (or perhaps one should say, with brains) distributed in their head and tentacles, these beings show a remarkable intelligence according to scientists, and they sometimes let themselves be tamed. However intelligent they might be, he mused, the above sea world with its forests, mountains, countryside and cities would remain forever concealed from them.

"To only rely on an intimate conviction is misleading and can even be fatal." Matthew said to Alex while they were rinsing their diving gear; then he added, "Some years ago, I had a test to which divers are sometimes subjected. They put me blindfolded in a big darkroom, with ear plugs for blocking noise, so that I had no reference. I had to walk ten steps forward, then ten steps backward while endeavoring to walk in a straight line, and I was asked to repeat this three or four times.

"And then?"

"Well, when they removed the blindfold, I had turned ninety degrees, although I was convinced not to have deviated"

"Yes," Alex replied, "convictions are more dangerous enemies of truth than lies…"

A little surprised, Matthew looked at Alex and said, "Nicely expressed…"

"The sentence is said to come from Nietzsche," admitted Alex with a smile, "and it suits me. It seems he had clearly identified the danger. I think too that convictions can be dangerous or even fatal. But intuitions are their cousin, and they seem essential to me. They are fleeting sunny intervals in the fog, and without claiming to be the truth, intuitions remain open and suggest potential paths."

7 - ITERATIONS

Just behind the door, at the bottom of the stairs, there was a switch. I pressed it, and the staircase filled with a faint glow. I climbed the first step, and not seeing where it was leading, I hesitated a moment. 'After all,' I said to myself 'when you are on a step, you can always climb up the next one...' The top of the stairs led to a corridor and as I progressed, arriving from a side corridor, I saw the woman that I used to think as 'my left neighbor' since I first saw her. We walked together without a word, and the corridor led to the door of a large hexagonal room. In the center of the room there was a circular table covered with a heavy white sheet down to the floor, and five chairs were arranged around it. Three of the chairs were already occupied, and the last two seemed to be waiting for us. We sat at the table. In its center, there was a basket of tasty fruits and a slate arranged vertically; on either side of it a strange message was written: '*You have held the rope and the control of your own fate begins with your freedom of speech.*'

For a few moments we looked at each other silently, and I realized that the four people that I could see around the table, two women and two men, were those who had been subjected to the strange halo phenomenon above their heads. But the halos were gone...

Then 'my left neighbor' raised her head, and hesitantly albeit with a cheerful tone, she uttered, "Well, I think that we are no longer subjected to the survival rules, and that we can talk as we wish."

We nodded in agreement and I spoke:

"I have no memory prior to the moment when I found myself at dinner in the great hall, three days ago. If I have a name, I think it could be Li-O.

One of the men replied, "I do not either have any recollection prior to that dinner, and I believe my name might be Osc-R."

'My left neighbor' said she believed to be named Laur-N, and then it was the turn of Lui-G and Agn-S. None of us had any memory previous to the first dinner.

"Why are we in this room?" asked Agn-S.

"Why… I do not know…" said Lui-G. "But thanks to… domino shaped reasoning, or rather a form of Russian dolls reasoning, I can explain how… All dolls are similar and fit together in one another. Once we have the first doll, one just needs to have the patience to go from one doll to the next, while fully maintaining the same reasoning structure, and in the end you get access to the final doll… the one that encompasses all the others…"

"Thus," he continued, "I knew that I had a halo above my head after the fifth announcement which said '*Some still remain…*' because I have reasoned as follows:"

- If there had been only *one* person with a halo and it was *not* me, then I would have seen one halo in the assembly.

But if the only person having a halo was me, I would not have seen any halo in the room. And, as the first announcement said that people having a halo had to leave, not seeing any I would have known that I had one and therefore had to leave.

Moreover, I had found a message in my room stating '*All guests in this place reason in the same way.*' Hence, in case of *one* halo *only*, anyone having the halo would have reasoned the same way, *and that person would have left after the first announcement.*

- If there had been only *two* persons with a halo and I was *not* one of them, then I would have seen two halos in the assembly.

But if I had been *one* of the two persons having a halo, I would have seen *only one* halo. However, as I just said, if the only halo I could see had been alone, he would have gone after the *first* announcement. Hence in case I had been *one* of the *two* only halos in the assembly, I would have gone after the second announcement. And the other person with a halo would have gone as well, since he would have reasoned the same way I do.

Then Agn-S continued the line of reasoning:

- If there had been only *three* persons with a halo and I was *not* one of them, then I would have seen three halos in the assembly.

But if I had been *one of* these three persons having a halo, I would have seen *only two* halos. However, as Lui-G just said, if the *two* halos I could see had been the *only two ones*, they would have gone after the *second* announcement. Hence, in case I had been *one* of the only three halos in the assembly, I would have gone after the *third* announcement. And the other persons with a halo would have gone as well, since they would have reasoned the same way I do.

Osc-R intervened:

"To sum up, because everybody follows the same line of reasoning, it has been shown that in the case of a single halo, whoever the person, he would have gone after the first announcement. In case of two halos, whoever the persons, they would have gone after the second announcement. In case of three halos, whoever the persons, they would have gone after the third announcement, and one can continue this way…"

- If nobody has left after the third announcement and I only see three halos, I can conclude that I have one, because otherwise the three others would already have gone. And in this case, I would leave after the fourth announcement.

"Finally, each of us five has noted at the fifth announcement that he could only see four halos, and therefore concluded that he had a halo over his head. The others, without a halo, have seen five halos in the assembly and have waited for the next announcement that will never come since they have no halo and we have left."

After a moment of silence Laur-N said, "I have used a similar reasoning***, but on a global level, and using a different language, and it also leads to the same conclusion…"

***The reasoning of Laur-N:*

-*"Let us suppose,"* she said, *"that there is a number of people N having a halo for which the following law applies: 'If there are N halos, then they will all leave after the N-th announcement.'*

At the moment, I do not know whether this number for which the law is true exists; but as a first step, I would like to show that if it were true when there are N halos, then it would also be true when there is one more halo i.e. N+ 1 halos.

In fact it is fairly quick:

- If I see N halos and indeed there are N, then assuming the law true for N, and according to that law, they should have left after the N-th announcement. But if they have not left after the N-th announcement, and I see N, I can conclude that in this case, I myself am carrying a halo, and we all leave after the next announcement i.e. the (N+1)-th announcement, since we all apply the same reasoning.

At this stage, I still do not know whether the law is true for N halos, but I have demonstrated that if it were true for a specific number of halos N, then it would also be true when there is N+1 halos (i.e. 1 more halo). However, and this is the second step of my line of reasoning, as shown by Lui-G, I know the law is true for one single halo who, not seeing any other one, would leave after the first announcement.

-But if the law is true for one halo, then as I have just demonstrated, it is also true for 1+1 halos i.e. two halos. But then, if the law is true for two halos, the law is also true for 2+1 halos and so on...

To sum it up: Since I have shown that if the law were true for N, then it would be also true for N+1, and since the law is true for N=1, the consequence is that it is actually true whichever the number N. In particular when N equals five, which is our case.

There was a silence after Laur-N's demonstration.

Then Agn-S said "This is all very interesting. Regardless of the language we have used, our logic has enabled us to get free from several constraints, but we still don't know what we are doing here, nor how to get out of this place."

"And what was the significance of these halos?" Laur-N murmured.

8 - ENTOMOLOGISTS

Matthew had returned to the office happy, for he had thoroughly enjoyed his trip with Alex. But, contrary to what he had hoped, his moments of solitary reflections on the sailboat had not provided him with specific ideas on how to address his mission. Over the hours, the benefits of the cruise faded quickly and, like a writer in front of his stubbornly blank page, he began to feel somewhat oppressed and to doubt whether he would be up to the task.

Leaning on the back of his chair, looking at his screen, he tried to struggle against the gloomy thoughts that pervaded him. He contemplated his screen, browsing the list of e-mails he had received during his absence. The title of one of them caught his attention. At first he thought it was a spam that had escaped the filtering software protecting his company from this kind of pollution. His name was indeed mentioned as the recipient, but the author's name did not appear. The title of the subject was:

'*Lateral thinking... Parallel thoughts... and Surrealism... often open the Way!*'

Normally he did not waste time to open such messages which he deleted without even reading them. But for some reason which he only understood in hindsight, he clicked. The text was as follows:

'*Subject: Lateral thinking... Parallel thoughts... and Surrealism... often open the Way!*

By looking well, it must surely be possible to notice an ant going out of Harvard University; but you will never see an ant coming out of this University with a diploma...

41

Still the future of ants seems much better assured than the human future...

Where is the flaw?

A. G.'

Matthew wondered what had prompted him to open this absurd e-mail. Upon reflection, it was the term 'Lateral thinking' mentioned in the subject line. Someone had recently used it in a conversation... It was not Alex during the cruise...

After a while, he remembered; the Boss had used such a wording when he had presented the project to him. He had referred to 'paving new ways' and 'lateral thinking'. Then he had told him not to cancel their cruise because it might prove useful 'to enter a lateral thinking mode.'

Could it be possible this message was a joke from the Boss?

This did not fit at all with his personality, and moreover the initials of the signature did not match... at least they did not match those of the Boss... Puzzled, Matthew decided to consider this as a sign sent to him by luck. He locked his office from inside, turned off his computer, and disconnected his phone. Then, comfortably ensconced in his chair tilted to the maximum, he let himself be pervaded by the rational or crazy thoughts that this message created in him...

After about an hour, he phoned Theresa and asked her if he could meet her in her office.

"Hymeno what?"

Theresa was looking at Matthew with both friendly and critical glances. She was the Human Resource Manager; she had medium long dark hair and a pleasant figure, and she gave an impression of friendly energy.

Matthew replied amused, "Hymenopterans: bees, ants, wasps... you know, these insects that live in organized colonies..."

Theresa was increasingly bewildered. She frowned, made a slight head movement of denial, and pretended to be worried. "You had too much partying last night, and you'd better rest... Unless I did not understand any of these management meetings I have been attending for so many years, I know for sure that our company does not produce honey, that we have nothing to do with 'desinsectization', and as far as I know, no entomological diversification is supposed to boost our sales. Anyway, I do not see how I could find someone among our colleagues who knows something about hyméno…pterans."

He laughed. "I did not party yesterday, and I am perfectly healthy, but sometimes one can be lucky. I know that you have access to the résumés of all the employees. So please kindly search all the CVs in house, since I would prefer somebody who already knows our company.

Theresa's phone rang just at the right moment, so that Matthew could slip away with a wave of his hand and without having to say more.

9 - MULTI-PATHS

I scrutinized the whole room. Apart from the door through which Laur-N and I had entered, and that through which Lui-G, Agn-S., and Osc-R had arrived, there did not seem to be any way out. The room did not include any windows, it was bathed in a soft light scattered by sconces located on each of the six walls.

Osc-R finished peeling a kiwi which he swallowed in one gulp. Visibly allured by the flavor of the fruit, he undertook to peel another one and said, "I don't know whether all this conforms to precise rules, but I suppose that we are not destined to remain forever in this room, and so there must be a way to get out." We all agreed.

"I hardly see any other way out than the two doors through which we entered," said Lui-G while walking towards the one that was closer to him. The door had closed after we had entered the room and it did not seem possible to open it from inside. Lui-G also checked that it was the same with the second door and added, "After all, this does not seem illogical; staying here or going back would neither be consistent with what has happened so far, nor with this imperious demand that we leave the place."

"Maybe..." answered Agn-S, "but the fact remains that there does not seem to be any way out."

At the same time, both Osc-R and Lui-G had the idea to scan the walls of the room. They were looking up and down and touched the areas within reach of their hands.

Suddenly Lui-G stepped back; he got closer to the wall and leaned to the right, then to the left, stepped back again and started again. Meanwhile, it seemed as though Osc-R had made an identical observation on the adjacent wall. They also inspected the other walls, but did not discover any other feature. Then each one returned towards his discovery, and they both engaged in a strange ballet. Placed in front of something that we could not perceive, they were alternating a step to the right and a symmetrical step to the left, to eventually refocus on their discovery, move one step back and start all over again. In doing so, they gradually progressed backwards to the center of the room. Arriving at mid-distance, they looked at us, and before they could utter a word, Laur-N said, "I agree with you, the exit is under the table."

We all began to move the heavy table, exposing a wooden hatch. Before opening it, Agn-S asked "How did you know?"

Osc-R answered,"Well, on one of the walls I have inspected, there is a thin strip in slightly different color... Or more exactly this strip reflects the light a little differently. If you are beside it you cannot see this, but if you stay right in front of it, you clearly notice it; and it remains noticeable even if you go away from the wall, as long as you can stay exactly facing it. Thus, while moving away from the wall, I was following a line perpendicular to the middle of the wall, which seemed to point to the centre of the room; I was realizing that it was the same with the adjacent wall for Lui-G, and that the two lines seemed to intersect in the centre of the room where the table is located. So, we both had an intuition that this was the place where we had to look."

Then I asked Laur-N how she had understood what Lui-G and Osc-R were doing, and guessed their conclusion.

"I had not guessed their conclusion and I had not understood what Osc-R and Lui-G were doing," she said, "at least until I had reached my own conclusion."

"How then did you know that the exit was under the table?"

"In fact it was not very difficult. It is the only place inaccessible to the eyes, and the whole visible part of the room seemed devoid of exits other than the two doors through which we entered and which are now locked..."

Then looking at our gawking faces, she smiled and added, "The path to knowledge is sometimes crooked, sometimes straight; but whatever the path, what matters is the end result..."

10 - ALOÏS

It was evening when Matthew parked his car in the street near his old friend Aloïs' home. In the old days when he was a student, a little by chance and a little out of curiosity, he had chosen an optional course entitled 'Philosophy of Science'. This course was attended by few students, and due to their limited number, it had taken the form of several informal discussions about the theory of knowledge in general, and about scientific methods in particular. The lecturer was an unusual character.

He was a philosopher scientist or perhaps the other way round... But he had not always been in an academic profession. He had spent much of his life creating new technologically oriented companies (the term start-up was not in use at the time), which he was eager to leave as soon as they had reached an industrial stage. Several of these companies were still active. Matthew knew that one of them had even become an international group, but Aloïs did not want to talk about it.

He had the remarkable and rare ability both to delve into very abstract theoretical reflections, as well as being capable of developing some of his ideas into their most practical consequences.

Some years after graduation, Matthew had incidentally met up with him again, and since then they had continued seeing each other even though it was too rarely.

Aloïs had now been retired for several years, but Matthew, as he had always been before, was delighted when they could meet. He was feeling a certain pride and was comforted to be friends with this man who used to look at nature and men with enlightened and slightly ironic eyes.

In the present time when vapid materialism, worshipping of immediacy, and pre-packaged 'Prêt à penser' generously distributed by media, try to prevail as compasses in a humanity without bearings, Matthew felt that he could find reasons for hope in Aloïs.

He briskly climbed three flights of stairs and rang the doorbell.

"Come in Matthew, the door is open," said the voice of Aloïs.

"Good evening, how did you know it was me?"

"Well I didn't hear the elevator before you rang the doorbell… It has been a while since you have come over"

There was no reproach in his voice; it was just an observation. Aloïs lived in a beautiful four-room apartment. The rustic furniture and decoration had been carefully chosen by his wife, when their resources had allowed it.

Since living alone, he had taken care of the apartment and its furnishings in memory of his wife, but he lived in a friendly mess which he called his 'functional chaos'. He was ensconced in a brown leather armchair. Next to it there was a pedestal table on which a book, a magazine, sheets of paper and some pens were placed. Not far from him, on a small wooden desk, the screen saver of the latest model laptop computer gleamed, witness and faithful servant of the old man's modernity and intellectual activity. Aloïs was holding a CD or a DVD without its cover, the surface of which reflected the iridescence of the split color light from the lamp.

"What brings you here?" he asked with a smile.

"The desire to spend some time with you…" and after a slight hesitation Matthew added, "… and perhaps a strange e-mail… but I think that I am disturbing you as you were about to put on a disc."

"No, no, I was just observing it…" replied Aloïs, still smiling.

11 - EXIT

We lifted the wooden hatch door, and a steep staircase appeared, as well as a switch. We went down one after the other, and after walking along a corridor of about thirty meters, we came to a door opening to the outside. From there a verdant path led to a wood.

Without knowing where we were going, or why, we began progressing along the path.

After about half an hour, the woods cleared, and when we reached the edge, we were at the foot of a large hill or perhaps a mountain. Being too close, we could not distinguish the summit. At the edge of the wood, the path branched off in two directions; to the left it seemed to run parallel to the base of the hill; to the right it gradually meandered up the hill.

We were perplexed, and sat down on the grass to decide what to do.

"We should go left," said Agn-S while chewing a blade of grass.

We were curious to know the reasons for her choice and understand what action to take. And we looked at her intensely, a little like students watching a professor who is about to reveal the knowledge they expected.

Then she stammered "Uh... yes, it's less tiring than climbing!" Although slightly disappointed, her embarrassment amused us.

"I believe instead, that we should take the path going up," I said

And, as if reading my thoughts, Laur-N said, "I agree with Li-O. If we follow the way down it will be easier; but leading where? We don't even know! While if we choose to climb, we might have a better vantage point. It could show us more about our situation."

Lui-G too was unwilling to walk up, but Osc-R agreed with us.

"So, what do we do?" said Laur-N.

Lui-G suggested we separate into two groups, but Agn-S did not share this view and preferred that we remain together. Lui-G reluctantly followed the majority opinion, and we took the path that gradually climbed the hill.

The path wound through the pines. Then, gradually they became rarer. We were now walking above a valley where a brisk stream flowed, and we could hear its murmur far away, attenuated by its distance…

12 - DVD

Matthew, somewhat taken aback, wondered about the interest of observing a DVD for such a long time with the naked eye.

"There are a few billion tiny dips and tiny bumps on the surface of this disk… Certainly, it constitutes a lot, but nevertheless it is a finite number," said Aloïs.

While he spoke, he dangled the disc under the lamp and, with fascination, stared at the small rainbow beams reflected by its surface.

Matthew did not see where Aloïs was going, but he did not interrupt him.

Aloïs turned to Matthew and said "This DVD is the film '*Gone with the Wind*'. *Have you seen it?*"

"Yes, long ago when I was a teenager… I remember a love story during the American Civil War with images of war and romance scenes."

"This is an old movie, made before the Second World War. This is the film, or at least one of the films, with the largest number of viewers in all of film history."

Then, Aloïs plunged back into the contemplation of the DVD's surface and, as if talking to himself, he continued, "In this plain disc, twelve centimeters in diameter, with all of its small dips and bumps, you have… the hair color of Scarlett, the cynicism of Rhett Butler, the smoke and sound of guns, the flames of the fires, the suffering and the blood of the wounded, the horrors of racism, the stupidity of war, the complexity of the feelings of love, the heroism of some and the cowardice of others… All in all, the beauty and ugliness, the greatness and smallness of the human condition…"

"Perhaps you could have chosen a more recent film," Matthew pointed out gently mocking.

Ignoring the remark, Aloïs continued, "What is surprising is that something so complex with all of these nuances can be digitized... As you know, all of this fits in a finite number of dips and bumps ranked in packets of eight (to which a few dips and bumps are adjoined for control)."

"Indeed." simply said Matthew.

"Hang on... Suppose we arrange every man and woman on earth in single file, and we provide each of them with a necklace of eight pearls to wear around their neck. Each of the pearls would be either white or black. If the selections of necklaces were properly made, then by interviewing people one after the other on the composition of their collar, one could achieve a structure having the same form as 'Gone With the Wind'; once decoded, this structure would include the same information as this DVD: the eyes and feelings of Scarlett, racism, war, etc."

"It's true," recognized Matthew, "after all, in spite of all the nuances contained in the movie, the number of basic information necessary to encode it, is large but not unimaginable."

"And if the arrangement and the proportion of each black and white eight-pearl necklace were properly changed, and people were questioned again successively on the composition of their collar, one could get the same structure and the same information as a DVD containing the film 'Titanic', to take a slightly more recent example..."

While listening, Matthew had gone towards the kettle, and had prepared a cup of tea for Aloïs and one for himself. Once again, he vaguely felt that his host was leading him towards one of those unexpected detours as he often did. However, a slightly off-key and incongruous thought made him smile, and he mumbled without even realizing it, "And what if the men do not want to wear necklaces?"

Aloïs had heard; with laughing eyes he replied, "If men do not want to wear necklaces, you just have to double the number of pearls on the ladies' necklaces... or else, offer them an additional bracelet with eight pearls. Hence neither in this respect would we be... irreplaceable!"

"It was just an attempt at 'lateral thinking'..." Matthew tried.

Aloïs did not react. He continued to think aloud.

"But information must be extracted. When I look at this disc with the naked eye, I see attractive colors, and it is already very beautiful. But if I want to know what it contains, I need what is called a player. In fact, it is rather a decoder, which detects and counts the dips, translates them and makes available all these amazing things. Maybe we will have the opportunity to talk about this another time…

Matthew realized he had arrived later than usual. He would have liked to continue the conversation, but he did not want to tire the old man. He apologized for the short duration of his visit, and then took leave, promising Aloïs, and promising himself, that he would come back and see him as early as he could.

Just before leaving, he asked, "Did you recently attempt to send me an e-mail?"

Aloïs simply answered "I get far too much pleasure in seeing you and hearing you to communicate via electronic mail…"

13 - CURIOSITY

After about two hours the slope became less steep, and we reached the top of the hill which offered a magnificent panorama to our eyes. The sun was still high above the horizon, and looking back, we could see all the way we had traveled. Down in the valley far away, we could distinguish the cloister and the adjoining wood where we came from. Ahead of us the path continued meandering down the hill to a plain, and in the distance we could perceive two constructions similar to the ones we had left, each of them being flanked by an adjoining wood.

We sat down on a bunch of rocks.

"What shall we do now?" asked Osc-R.

"The question should be rather 'What do we want to do'," Agn-S replied.

"Or else 'What are we *supposed* to do?... Are we masters of our fate, or is it pre-determined, perhaps even written...?" Laur-N wondered aloud.

"I have the impression that we are all haunted by these pressing questions, and that each of us feels the urge to know why he or she is here, what to do, and where all this is going." Lui-G said.

"Then we do not really have a choice," I pointed out.

Pointing to the two buildings in the distance, Osc-R agreed "Yes, we need to see what's going on down there."

Yet Lui-G said, "We managed to get out of what looked like a rather comfortable prison. I would rather not be held again in another prison which might even be worse than the previous one."

"Indeed," I said, "it's a risk, but what are we to do? Wander over hill and dale haphazardly, not knowing where to go? Moreover, even if none of us for the moment seems to feel hungry, thirsty, or tired, who knows whether or not we will have to take our basic needs into account in the near future?"

"Well, how do we proceed? Shall we go there together, or shall we part, asked Agn-S?"

And she added, "It would be more comfortable to stay together, but on the other hand, we will then have to visit two cloisters one after the other; it will take more time, and be less discreet than if we were in small groups."

We walked down the lane, and arrived at a place which separated into three branches. The left branch and the right branch both appeared to lead to one of the cloisters. It was decided that Laur-N and I would take the left path, and the others would take the right path. According to what we had seen from the top of the hill, we reckoned there was still about half an hour's walk to each of the cloisters. We agreed to meet at the site of the junction, at dusk at the latest; those arriving first would wait for the others.

The path ran along the wood, and as we walked, Laur-N pointed out that we had not met anyone, men or animals, since being out in the open.

Gradually, as we were approaching the cloister, a sense of oppression came over us as if we were heading back to a world where we would not control our destinies. We arrived at the cloister. The main gate was closed, and walking along the outside wall, we reached a heavy wooden door. To our surprise, it was not locked.

The door opened directly onto a staircase, and we had no other choice than to climb it or to turn back. The staircase was dimly lit, and as we were climbing, oppression changed into anguish. We were wondering whether we would find ourselves again confined in a place where everything would be imposed on us and which we would no longer be able to leave.

We arrived at what seemed to be the top of the building, and the staircase led to a small room furnished with two armchairs and a table. On it, there were fruits, meats, cheeses, salad and bread. At the back of the room there was a small curtain and a door. After having unsuccessfully tried to open the door, Laur-N drew back the curtain, unveiling the only window of the room. But the window was facing the interior of the building, overlooking a huge room. Its floor was located about ten meters below, and its ceiling was at the same level as the ceiling of the room we were in.

"Come and see," Laur-N said in a trembling voice.

I approached, and was chilled by what I could see.

Suddenly we were overcome by an irresistible urge to sleep, and both of us collapsed into the armchairs in the room.

14 - HIVES

It was nine o'clock in the morning, Matthew arrived at the office in a bad mood, grumbling about the traffic jams that wasted two hours of his life per day and added to his daily stress. Ruminating these negative thoughts, he entered his office without noticing the person seemingly waiting for him in the hallway. He had just sat down when he heard a knock at the door. And although the intonation of the "Yes?", which Matthew blurted, had sounded rather like a "No!" a young woman entered the room. She was dark, her curly hair framing a regular featured face with high cheekbones, green eyes with a deep look, and a dazzling smile. In front of such a celestial appearance, Matthew's aggressiveness disappeared as if by magic.

"What can I do for you?"

"Good morning," she said, "my name is Chloe, and Theresa asked me to come and see you. Strangely, Theresa has added, 'You are not an entomologist, but I think you can meet his expectations, and perhaps even better than he hoped'."

"Then sit down and tell me everything..."

"After a PhD in Computer Science, three years ago I was hired by our company to work on the analysis and the design of computation software for some of our large customers. But for some time, my work has evolved to software focused on supporting the management of large organizations.

Although he appreciated her calm and energetic voice, Matthew thought about all of his work, and that this person in the end had a resume relatively common within the company.

He asked her abruptly, "What do you know about hymenopterans?"

Undaunted, she replied almost merrily, "Not much..."

Matthew was about to put an end to the discussion when she said, "Not much from a biological point of view, but a little more on the behavioral level. During my studies, I was led to work on computer modeling of bee's behavior in a hive. Each of the bees was regarded as an individual having no idea of the common objective or purpose of the collective hive, but endowed with a minimum of basic elementary 'programmed' behaviors, allowing it to fulfill its role within the hive.

Matthew relaxed, and leaning on the back of his chair he murmured, "Tell me…"

"Well, several studies have already been conducted in order to reproduce the behavior of an anthill. On the same principle, the virtual ants were programmed to react to situations in their virtual environment with simple behaviors. For example, simulating an ant's stroll, if it encountered food, regardless of the size of the object, it would position itself so that the object was between it and the nest, and it would begin to push. If the object was too heavy, it would continue to push, even if this had no effect. But if such an ant met a congener already busy pushing an object, it was programmed to go to the same side and also push. And the process continued so that after a while, the virtual ants were sufficiently numerous to begin to move the object towards the anthill. With a relatively limited number of individual programmed behaviors, such as those I just described, or for example, one in which each ant leaves a temporary trace on the path it has followed, which in reality corresponds to a kind of odor, it has been possible to replicate the behavior of an anthill rather closely."

"So were you dealing with ants or bees?"

"I worked on bees using the same principles, applied to little more complicated social behaviors. The idea was to determine the minimum number of programmed elementary behaviors made available to each individual that would enable the whole group (the hive in the case of my work) to function."

"Did it work?"

"Yes," she replied simply. Then she added, "By modeling in this manner, with "multi-agent systems" as we call them in our jargon, we reached some interesting results. It was shown that a so-called "emergent behavior" of the hive appears. Although none of the agents (I mean the bees) have the overall plan, or even the general vision of the hive, everything goes as if the hive was an organism whose purpose is to organize its own survival and reproduction."

"And you're still working on this subject?"

"No, after my studies I had to earn a living, and I started working here on other matters."

"How would you like to pursue the matter again?"

She had a big smile, and again Matthew was charmed.

"Yes, certainly, but why do you want to study bees? Are you interested in this issue?"

"Not really… but bees probably have much to contribute…"

15 - TRIGGER

When I woke up, Laur-N was still asleep in the other armchair. The top button of her blouse was open, and I could see a necklace made of several black and white pearls at the base of her neck.

She soon opened her eyes. Our first instinct was to look through the window. Nothing had changed, and the scene remained the same.

Down in the hall, about fifty guests were sitting at different tables, apparently at the beginning of their meal, but what made the scene grim and frightening was that all the people had frozen into complete immobility, and that nothing had changed since we had entered the room.

"In your opinion how long have we been here?" I asked Laur-N.

"I have no idea. We have been asleep, but apparently nothing happened to us."

"That's true, but we have not yet emerged from here…"

We were probably hungry because we sat at the table without even thinking about it.

"Is this staged? Are all the people down below statues?" asked Laur-N.

Then she added, "This immobility is frightening. If it were up to me, I would give them the means to move."

She got up and went back to the window, cast a glance, then calmly returned to the table and began to peel an apple; and looking at me she whispered in a voice slightly choked, "They have begun to move."

I looked through the window. Down below in the hall, the guests had started their meals served by a couple of young waiters; all of this in absolute silence.

As I returned to the table, the door located next to the window, which had resisted previous attempts by Laur-N, suddenly opened. The waitress came into the room, took three steps toward us, stopped and silently looked at us. She was the same waitress who had served us before we came out of the cloister… or her double. There was neither hostility, nor benevolence in her gaze, just a kind of polite indifference.

As the silence dragged on, Laur-N tried "Good morning Madam." Before she could add anything, the young woman with a half-smile, tilted her head forward and said, "Good morning Madam, good morning Sir." She then walked out in the same way as she came, closing the door behind her.

I rushed after her, but the door would not open. Through the window, we saw the waitress talking to one of the guests, then to another; these guests began talking to their neighbors, and soon the hall was filled with polite and scarcely enlivened conversation snippets.

Not knowing what to do, we finished our meal, and after a while I asked Laur-N, "And now?"

"I think we have nothing left to do here, we'd better try to join the others?"

"It would be surprising if they had the patience to wait for us, because we have probably been here for several hours."

Laur-N, checked that the door through which we had entered the room opened freely. Before leaving, we decided to explore every corner of the small room.

After a last glance through the window, just in case, I inspected the back side of the curtain, and what I saw astounded me.

16 - PSY

Matthew gazed absently at his computer screensaver. He had first seen it at Aloïs' place, who had given him a copy of the file at his request. As he was handing him the copy, Aloïs had said, "It's weird, copying this file has given me a headache... My computer crashed and rebooted twice while I was making it..."

Matthew had it checked out by his company's Computer Department. The small software did not contain any viruses, and it met all the safety standards. The Department had no objections; hence Matthew had installed it on his computer.

A small stylized computer was moving across his screen, on the screen of the stylized computer was another small computer moving, the latter showing a computer moving... and so on. If the cursor was placed on the screen of the moving computer, with a zoom effect, it would take up all the space on the actual screen. The following moving screen would take the place of the previous one. One could do so indefinitely... At each step the screen changed colors, and the moving computer changed shape.

Matthew remembered the insistence of the Boss' words, '...*The project must remain absolutely secret; you need to find a way to have teams working together without knowing the final goal. Of course, as the project progresses, some of your colleagues should be made aware. It is your responsibility to decide who and when...*'

He turned off his webcam. Due to a widespread and apparently unresolved bug, it had the bothersome habit of switching on each time the computer was started. It was not dramatic, but he found it somewhat irritating...

He picked up his phone and dialed Alex's number.

"Would you be available to lunch with me tomorrow by noon?"

"With pleasure, but not to talk about work. I have a rather busy day tomorrow, and I am going to want to relax a bit."

"Sure, no problem with that," Matthew lied shamelessly.

He had two reasons for wanting to talk to Alex privately: one involved Alex and the project, and the other involved the project... and Alex's wife.

Then he visited Theresa.

She greeted him with a smile, "So? Have you had time to interview the virtual entomologist that I sent you?" she asked.

"Yes, congratulations, you did a great job; I was looking for someone exactly like her," Matthew replied with a little more enthusiasm than he intended.

He knew Theresa who, by nature and by function, was not easily fooled. And as he did not want to get into explanations about the work he had to do, he directly addressed the subject of his visit.

"As far as I know, we do not use a corporate psychologist, do we?"

"No, but we have a dedicated office to whom we entrust assignments or seminar organizations. When we need to build up highly cohesive teams, or when we need to motivate certain services or key elements in our organization, we use them."

"And it works?"

"Sometimes yes, sometimes no; it's hard to say... It is often difficult to get an idea of the effectiveness of these missions. On the one hand we need someone who can objectively judge the needs of the company and, in this case, the person must be external to the company. On the other hand, it requires someone with intimate knowledge of the company and its intricacies, not only in its explicit but also in its implicit organization... But what do you need? Are there problems in your department? Or are these personal problems?"

"No, no... I am trying to build a team for a major project..."

"Do you want to set up a kind of 'Team Building' session in order to bring cohesion to the team?"

"Actually I'm seeking someone to permanently integrate into the team."

Theresa put her elbow on the armrest of her chair and, with her chin resting on her fist, she looked Matthew straight in the eyes.

"This is the first time that I have had such a request... Will you not tell me more?"

"It's somewhat complicated, and I still need to think a little more before I can clarify what I am looking for…"

Theresa appreciated Matthew and his effectiveness. He was naturally assertive, and unlike many of his colleagues, he did not need to be arrogant to look competent. Since she was tactful she did not insist, and Matthew went to see Rudy.

17 - REACTION

Laur-N was inspecting the underside of the table where we had eaten, and I heard my voice falter when I told her, "Laur-N, there is a text embroidered in red thread on the inside of the curtain,"

"And what is written there?" she asked, without stopping her own inspection.

I read the first sentence aloud: *"Those who cannot see their own halo, will leave before tomorrow night, otherwise they will disappear."*

And as I was pronouncing these words, I could clearly hear the sound of my own voice transmitted to the large room below.

After the first moment of surprise, she asked, "Is that all?"

"No, there are additional sentences."

"What do they say?"

"There are still some who have to leave- and then three times - *Some still remain…"* I whispered.

The door, which had provided access to the hall and through which the waitress had entered, was locked again. We had no alternative but to go down the stairs and to get out of the cloister.

The sun was rising on the horizon in the fresh morning air, and we were walking along the woods. Thus, we had spent the night in the cloister.

Laur-N asked as if talking to herself, "Through your voice, they heard the first instruction embroidered on the curtain concerning their halos. Who is going to read the other instructions to them?"

I did not know. Maybe they were intended to be read by other visitors.

Again we reached the junction of the three paths and found neither Osc-R, nor Agn-S, nor Lui-G.

After some hesitation over the action to be taken, we decided somewhat reluctantly, to go and see whether our companions were stuck in the other cloister. The path was much like the one we had followed the day before. However, we were unable to enter the building because all of its entrances were locked.

A little worried about their fate, we had no choice but to return to the junction and explore the third path. After about an hour, it led to a deserted asphalt road.

It could have been about noon when we heard a buzzing noise behind us, hardly perceptible at first, then louder. We saw a bus coming towards us. As it was approaching, it slowed down.

18 - EXTRACTION

Matthew was in Rudy's office, facing him. He was talking about a knowledge extraction project.

"I have some general ideas on the matter," Rudy was saying, "but I'm far from being an expert. In fact I'm not even sure that it is very clear in my mind."

They decided to seek help from Alex. Matthew knew that Alex was fairly busy, but he let Rudy call him. They put their conversation on speakerphone.

"*Data extraction* also called *data mining*", Alex's voice was saying, "means to bring to light, in a presentable form, useful information such as statistics, correspondence, and correlations, by searching databases where these data are stored in considerable numbers. But within such data warehouses, data are by nature structured, factual and often digital."

"And *knowledge extraction*?" asked Rudy.

"*Knowledge extraction* also means finding relevant information among huge amounts of data, and presenting it in a useful way. But it is no longer confined to exploiting structured databases; it also seeks to use all relevant data wherever they are... For example in plain language texts, or in images, provided these data are accessible by computer, as is the case with the Internet, or company networks."

"So in the case of knowledge extraction, we dig into enormous quantities of data even if they are not structured in specific warehouses..."

"That is correct," Alex concluded.

Then decidedly in a hurry, he said, "I am sorry but I must leave you now, I really don't have time..." and he hung up.

Rudy and Matthew remained silent for a moment. After a while, Rudy declared "We cannot reinvent the wheel... If I understand correctly, you are asking me to build a team in order to develop a *knowledge extraction* system, capable of merging data from various sources. These sources will have nothing to do with each other, neither in their content, nor in their format, nor in purpose. And the system should be able, upon each query, to make a summary report on the subject…"

"While allowing, if necessary, to monitor the path that led to the report," Matthew completed.

"And you know, as well as I do, that although internally we have some experience in *data mining*, what you are asking for is a different story."

Someone knocked at the door, and a smiling secretary brought the mail. As she let herself out, Rudy let a dreamy look wander on the rolling gait of the young high-heeled woman. Then, going through the motions, he adjusted his dark-red tie, and after having thought for a while he continued, "There are several companies already mulling over the problem. The best way to proceed would be to know what is happening elsewhere on this very subject. Maybe we could allocate a budget to go and steal some others' secrets…"

Rudy was in his thirties. He was a smiling man with early graying hair and a slight tendency to be overweight. He had a sharp mind and was a brilliant tactician, but in spite of the friendly expression on his face, he was totally impervious to any ethical or moral consideration if it related to business or to his career.

In this respect he was a caricature of what elite schools can produce when ethical issues are regarded as a kind of politically correct cosmetic, attached to certain lessons in order to keep up appearances.

Matthew had the feeling that this cynical trend was increasing in the business world as well as in politics and media; and he found this distasteful…

The very nature of the professional environment in which he was operating, forced him to position himself with respect to these trends. Thus, he had come to construct his own philosophy.

He wanted to think, while shaving every morning in front of his mirror, that although every being has a dark side, he behaved as an 'honest man'. But he did not know whether indeed he was one… And actually, do mirrors allowing this kind of reflection exist?

Admittedly, out of pragmatism, for reasons of efficiency, and perhaps also for comfort, he stood by a certain number of values and behaviors he deemed important. However, he did not blindly adhere to official moral doctrines, as he found they were often too close to self-righteous conformism.

This way of thinking and of self-conduct had imposed itself upon him over the years; and experience had taught him that even if a naively direct attitude could sometimes appear initially unsuccessful, all in all, in the end, honest behaviors were more 'profitable' than dishonest ones.

To speak in a financial language, he had realized that on medium and long term, the 'return on investment' of straightness was higher than that of deception.

As a matter of fact, he preferred to believe that he was interested in morals, rather than to think he was moral out of interest… but sometimes there was a remaining doubt…

"What do you think?" insisted Rudy.

Matthew thought it was not worth trying to explain to him why he did not want to release a specific budget in order to spy on competitors. Rudy probably would not have understood…Thus he only answered, "No, we do not have enough money for this kind of operation; but I agree with you, we cannot reinvent the wheel"

"So?"

"So, I suggest you find everything in the public domain that exists on the subject, and then investigate whether, with our in-house expertise, we can set something up."

"And you think this is going to take us far?"

"I do not know if it will be enough to start the process, but once we have a preliminary idea, if necessary, we will hire some experts to help us."

"We will have to poach these folks from somewhere…" Rudy murmured.

"Not necessarily, there may be independent talents in the market; but if it is necessary, and if they want to come and work here with us, then why not?"

"And who is the customer?" asked Rudy abruptly.

"I do not know, I do not even know if it's an internal request or an external order," replied Matthew.

Rudy was not convinced by Matthew's answer, but he did not show it.

19 - CITY

The bus arrived at our level, stopped, and the front door opened. Laur-N looked at me quizzically. Just like me, she hesitated to climb in the bus. The driver turned to us. He looked exactly like the waiter who had served us in the cloister. He said calmly, "Well? What are you waiting for? We're already late…"

The driver did not look hostile, and we had nothing better to do…So we got into the bus. It was almost full, with the exception of a two seats next to each other marked 'N' and 'O' where we sat, and the bus drove off. The passengers were dozing, or talking quietly. A kind of numbness came over us.

Laur-N rooted around in the pocket located on the back of the seat in front of her, and pulled out what appeared to be a map of a small city. There was nothing in the pocket facing my seat.

The bus drove for about an hour, and then we arrived in an urban area. In fact, it looked more like a large campus than a city. It was made up of small buildings a few floors high. They were clean looking, if somewhat impersonal. The buildings were separated by small green spaces, intersected by roads and paths.

Then the bus came to a parking area and stopped. The central door opened and we heard the driver's voice, still as calm as ever, saying through the speaker, "End of the line, everybody off the bus. Thank you for traveling with us." After a moment of hesitation, the passengers got out of the bus and dispersed in all directions.

"What happens now, Laur-N wondered aloud?"

"I do not know…We are totally unaware of the laws to which we are subjected …We do not even know where we come from… How can we find out where we are going?" I replied morosely.

20 - APPLE

Absorbed in his thoughts, Matthew returned to his office.

As he absently glanced at his computer, he realized that the screen saver had frozen. The image of the small computer was still there, but it was fixed. Instead of displaying a succession of other computers on its screen, it displayed the number ' 01000110 '. Matthew clicked several times on the image, but nothing happened. Given it could be a computer error code, he scribbled it on a piece of paper. In a final attempt, he clicked again for a few seconds, and the letters "A. G." appeared instead of the code. Then everything returned to normal, and the small moving computers resumed their course. Contemplating the sequence of zeros and ones, Matthew embarked on a mini calculation and concluded that this was the expression of the number 70 in the binary numbering system…After all, it probably did not matter, and he would talk to the Technical Services at some point. But without really knowing why, the incident made him think of Aloïs; probably because he had given him the screensaver software. Perhaps, he could offer him some insight about it. He was always delighted to see the old professor, and it would be a good opportunity to visit him again later in the day.

When Matthew arrived at his place, Aloïs was busy reading a book while crunching an apple, with apparently great pleasure. Matthew noticed that he was using the DVD "Gone With The Wind" as a bookmark

As he inquired about his health, Aloïs declared, "I guess at my age, it is quite normal not to be on the rise. My doctor has decided that a nurse should come to see me once a week. Do not worry, nothing serious. But still…"

Then, much to Matthew's surprise, he added with a slight wink,

"The only good aspect of the matter is that she is absolutely charming!" Matthew, a little uncomfortable, preferred to change the subject.

"Last time we spoke, you mentioned readers and decoders to extract information from the DVD"

"Yes, that's correct, he replied soberly."

But apparently returning to his first subject, he said on a light tone, "When two bodies attract each other, they have three possible behaviors: either each of them deviates from its route but continues its way, or they begin to revolve around each other, or else both bodies fall one on the other."

Furtively, a female figure came back to Matthew's memory, and against his will, one of the three options became substantially more distinct in his thoughts than the others.

"In addition," Aloïs continued, "the closer they get to each other, the stronger their mutual attraction"

'*It's true! But why talk about this?*' thought Matthew.

He knew Aloïs had an eclectic mind. However, his remark about the nurse, as well as the anthropology of romantic behavior that he seemed keen to address in their discussion, appeared to be off key with respect to his usual restraint and elegance.

Could it be that, under the influence of age, some demons were waking up belatedly? Prudent, he did not say anything, and waited with a mixture of curiosity and apprehension.

"There is a universal language in which nature expresses itself..."

The remainder was pending. The topic and the silence that followed the words of Aloïs were becoming embarrassing. Matthew wriggled uncomfortably in his chair, and felt an unpleasant sensation of heat pervading him. He tried to break the silence as neutrally as possible.

"A language of nature, or a communication language that humans have invented to express natural behavior?"

The reply of Aloïs did not provide an answer, and even increased his discomfort.

"Of all the natural constraints that apply to us, there is one which is my favorite, wonderful in its depth, simplicity and even gravity."

Matthew watched Aloïs stealthily. Yet, he did not look like a tormented old man. Pointing at the basket full of fruit, the latter offered, "Do you want an apple? They come directly from the producer, and they are delicious."

The offer was tempting; it provided a diversion, and Matthew agreed.

Aloïs swiftly grabbed the fruit, and threw it to his friend. After having followed a nice parabolic course, the apple landed directly into Matthew's funnel positioned hands.

"The laws of nature are expressed in mathematical language…" said Aloïs. His tone became a little more like a professor's when he pursued, "Yes, in mathematical language! And although the idea already existed in the embryonic stage among the Greeks, the man who seemed to have really become aware of this, or at least explicitly formulated it first, lived a long time ago. He was called Galileo, and he was right. We have not found any better ways than the mathematical language to express the fundamental laws of nature."

Matthew suddenly felt the atmosphere become lighter. It was probably the first time in his life a topic that might well be heavy, even boring, deprived him of the burden of a light discussion. Still Aloïs continued, "One can wonder whether this language is only a means invented by mankind to communicate. However, it seems that it is more than just a communication language."

"Why is that?

"It not only allows communicating about nature, but also it makes it possible to decrypt it… But let us come to this natural law, whose depth, gravity and simplicity captivate me, and which Mr. Newton discovered. What does it say?

It says that if you want to know the force exerting between two bodies, you have to multiply the mass of one of them by that of the other, divide it by the square of the distance between them, and multiply all this by a constant which, as its name suggests, is a number that does not depend on the situation observed."

He grabbed a magazine from the pedestal table and scribbled on the cover: $F = k\,(\,M \times m\,)\,/\,d^2$.

"Voila! This simple law allows one to know the force acting between two bodies due to their mass alone. Complemented by two other laws, just as simple, and with a little math within reach of a second-year science student, it also predicts the motion of two bodies relative to each other."

"Thus it is not a matter of calculating their hormone levels, as you might have thought a moment ago," he added with an amused smile.

Of course, Aloïs had to be aware that this was well known to Matthew… The latter, definitely reassured about Aloïs, and although not knowing on what paths he was being led, was finally able to relax and continue the discussion.

"Treaties on physics are filled with multitudes of formulae, more or less complicated; why so much enthusiasm for this one?"

"What is extraordinary", said Aloïs, "is that this law seems to apply, let's say… for the sake of the legend, between an apple, like that I have thrown you, and the Earth. But it also works between the Moon and the Earth, as well as between the Earth and the Sun. Then it was realized that it was working between the different stars that form a galaxy, and also between the galaxies themselves. As far as we can observe the universe, this law seems to describe what happens from the perspective of gravity."

"But what is it that specifically fascinates you?" Matthew insisted.

"What amazes me", said Aloïs, is the accuracy and universality of the formula, and that, in our primate brains, we could uncover a formula of such precision and such universality. By the way it's a truism to say that this law cannot be better named, since everyone knows it as the 'Law of Universal Gravitation'… *To me, this is the first law, later followed many others, that allowed humans to project beyond the universe in which they lived.*"

"So it is of historical interest…"

"Not only… This formula is a gateway to other worlds… It is as if one day, after having studied the surrounding water, and after deep reflection, a group of tropical marine fish had predicted the existence of glaciers, snow, and rivers…"

This time it was the Mahon octopus that briefly came back to Matthew's mind. Perhaps, after all, in a few hundred thousand years, evolution would allow octopuses' "distributed brain" to get an idea of the emerged world.

After a moment of silence, Aloïs conceded, "Although this law has appeared extremely accurate during centuries, in fact, to be really precise, one must take into account relativistic corrections made later by another famous character named Einstein… Thus mankind got access to a formulation of the law of gravity apparently really universal."

"The relativistic corrections make the formulation very complex," Matthew noted.

"Yes, and for the rest of the story we will restrict ourselves to the simple formula of Newton, the accuracy of which remained for a long time without being faulted."

Matthew wondered, half-worried, half amused, what story Aloïs was referring to when he mentioned the continuation to come... He had passed the age of physics courses!

But Aloïs continued, "The knowledge of all these physical laws, that mankind has been able to uncover and express in an appropriate language, not only allowed human beings to discover the secrets of nature, but also to cope with it. Humanity has achieved incredible things, such as getting rid of day and night, overcoming the laws of gravity, talking and seeing each other remotely, getting access to forces millions times more powerful than animal power..."

"Still it does not seem that it makes men and women happier", muttered Matthew.

"Correct, but that is another problem, for which there is currently no mathematical formulation... even taking into account hormone levels..."

"But what about the DVD decoder?"

21 - ACCOMMODATION

While undertaking to unfold the map that she had found on the bus and still had in her hand, Laur-N muttered, "Okay we do not know where we have come from or where we are going, or what laws govern this place, but perhaps we can at least know where we are."

Indeed the bus parking area was represented on the map, and in addition, an itinerary had been traced from the point where we were located and led to a building on Dee Cartes Street, about two kilometers away.

We set off. There was little traffic, and the walk up to Dee Cartes Street was nice. We reached the foot of the building, and the front door was locked with a digicode. The building had three floors, and for each floor there were eight doorbell buttons identified by a letter.

For the third floor, the eight buttons were labeled I through P. After several unsuccessful attempts, we entered the letters N and O on the keypad and the building's front door opened. Reaching the third floor, we found ourselves facing eight doors, divided into two rows of four. They ran along each of the two main facades of the building. Each door was designated by the same letter as its doorbell, but without strictly adhering to the normal alphabetical order. Doors N and O opened smoothly.

I entered the apartment O, and Laur-N entered the other.

Both through its arrangement and furniture, the apartment was different from the one where I had spent the first three nights of my... 'existence' or 'adventure'. (How does one describe what had happened to me since I had been offered some salad in the cloister's dining room?) Yet, for a brief moment, I felt as if I were back in the cloister. It did not last, but a vague feeling of anxiety persisted inside of me.

There was a short corridor, a few meters long leading to a living room, giving access to a bedroom and an adjoining bathroom. In the bedroom as well as in the living room, a window allowed guests to contemplate the outdoor greenery and the other buildings. The bedroom included a closet furnished with linen and men's clothes, a large bed with two bedside tables, and a desk with a chair. In the living room there was a table surrounded by six chairs, a sofa, two cozy armchairs, and a kitchenette containing a fridge full of food. The floor was covered with plush beige carpet. I walked over to the bathroom, and I could see my own image in the mirror. Then my anxiety disappeared.

I looked tired… and I could see that, around my neck, the necklace was made of eight black and white pearls.

22 - ISOMORPHISM

Aloïs had ignored the question, or perhaps he had not heard it. He pursued his idea.

"What is amazing is that the mathematical language has a unique feature. Not only, like other languages, will it allow description and communication, but it also acts as a filter because its structure forbids formulating propositions contradicting one another. If common languages are all-terrain vehicles that allow one to go on any path of imagination, mathematical language is a process that builds its rails as and when it progresses. One can choose to move with the train, but one does not know where the railway, which is being built, will actually lead."

He paused.

"So what about the DVD decoder?" repeated Aloïs, who had after all heard Matthew's question. "Well…" he continued, "as you know, the development, or rather the discovery of this language so well suited to the laws of nature, took centuries and centuries, requiring efforts, errors, and successes of thousands of brilliant people, usually throughout a lifetime. Since the prehistoric era, over the generations, there has been a series of hundreds of geniuses. Each generation has added and sometimes cut off (for the progress of science is far from having followed only an upward curve) an additional layer in the way of thinking as well as in the way of using brains of people who had access to knowledge."

His somewhat professorial tone had disappeared; Matthew was silent and watched with pleasure the old man's face come to life under the influence of passion. He looked like a gourmet describing his favorite cake.

"A little," he continued, "as if, over generations, the pooling and sharing of thoughts from all those brains was building the decoder necessary to understand nature and the universe. And even those who have not had access to this knowledge have benefited (or sometimes suffered) from the resulting progress of this understanding."

Aloïs concluded, "We are far from having completed the construction of this decoder... But, if humanity does not self-destruct beforehand, thanks to this ongoing pooling and sharing of the discoveries of all these brains, one can imagine that future generations will penetrate the deepest secrets of the universe in which mankind is immersed."

He seemed tired now, and it made him look as if he doubted the optimistic part of the alternative he had just mentioned.

It was time to leave. But, looking him straight in the eyes, Aloïs said, "You know, this young nurse is really charming..." Again Matthew felt embarrassed and got nervous. But Aloïs continued, "I do not usually play matchmaker, but I really wish to introduce her to you; I have the feeling that you have lost the "joie de vivre" you used to have, and that you need to see people... Matthew smiled; indeed, Aloïs noticed everything.

"Do not worry about me, I have many friends and I go out a lot," he lied. Then he showed Aloïs the piece of paper where he had written the sequence "01000110", and explained the circumstances in which it had appeared on his screen saver. Aloïs gave it a quick glance, and without even thinking, he replied "It's the number 70 written in binary notation." He did not seem to attach great importance to this issue, but strangely he added, "I don't see what else can be said about it, but if it happens again, please let me know."

As Aloïs walked him to the door, Matthew could not help but ask him one last question.

"So the universe is the DVD, and the human brain is the decoder?"

"No... the decoder is what the emergent system, made of brains communicating with each others, is capable of creating... And in fact, the human decoder is even more fabulous than the DVD decoder. Just like the DVD decoder, it provides a vision of existing things, even though they are invisible and inexorably hidden to the naked eye, and even though the story revealed by this decoder is still developing in real time (at least from our perspective)."

He also added, "It reveals isomorphisms as well..."

Matthew went down the stairs meditating on this cryptic sentence and, in spite of himself, also thinking a little about Aloïs' nurse...

23 - POINT SQUARE

The next day we decided to explore our new environment and to walk towards a central square shown on the map called Point Square. We thought that because of its location, it might be a natural crossroads and therefore probably a lively place.

We were wandering quietly (and for the first time without worrying) in a large tree-lined avenue when our attention was drawn to a poster attached to one of them. It was a small poster; maybe a local resident had lost something and hoped that someone from the neighborhood had seen it or collected it.

Out of curiosity, we approached the tree. Laur-N was the first one to get close. After a quick glance she turned to me, and again I saw anxiety written on her face. She stepped aside to let me read the five words followed by an ellipsis written on the poster, '*Those who, through their efforts…*'

We continued our journey in silence, and a little further, another poster appeared on a tree, on which was written, '*…will firmly hold the rope…*' Further, a third poster continued '*Soon shall master their fate…*' And as we expected it, just before arriving in the square, a fourth poster ended the motto '*…and be able to cope*'

The square was rectangular. The cafés scattered on its edges, as well as the lawn and the fountain located in its center, should have made the place pleasant and conducive to relaxation. Yet a heavy atmosphere reigned. People spoke very little, or in a low voice, and the way they walked was not that of careless onlookers. While apparently moving aimlessly, they seemed to be waiting for something.

A small crowd near the fountain drew our attention. At the center of the fountain, there was a bronze statue depicting an unclothed young woman, sitting on a sphere wedged in between two large books. She held in her right hand raised to shoulder height, what appeared to be a stylus. In her left hand there was a tablet resting on her knee, at which she seemed to stare. Along the equator of the sphere, we could see eight groups of eight white or black glossy colored tiles; they were in a single line and without any apparent regular pattern.

On the circular rim of the fountain was engraved the phrase '*Thank you for responding to this invitation*'.

As if this sentence was directly addressed to us, I could not help saying to Laur-N, "Did we really have a choice?"

A little farther on the edge of the fountain, there was another sentence, 'Observe constantly.'

"Maybe these are clues on how to discover the laws that govern us..." she suggested.

In the middle of a group, we could distinguish Lui-G, and we also saw Agn-S and Osc-R. Without lecturing them, Lui-G was addressing the group of people around him, and we could hear bits of phrases interspersed with ambient murmurings "... *shows the way... we must obey...what is good for us... seek to understand...*" people listened quietly, some nodded assent, some on the contrary did not seem to agree, others were without reactions, however everyone remained quiet.

Osc-R and Agn-S greeted us with a smile.

"We were worried about you because we were waiting for you at the agreed place in vain," said Agn-S.

She then began to tell us of their visit to the cloister.

"Only one door seemed to open, and a staircase led to the top floor of the building. We entered a room with a window overlooking the main hall where two waiters were busy with fifty guests silently eating. In the room where we were, there was a table with three plates, chairs, and an apple on each plate, which we eagerly ate because we were hungry. While we were perplexed and wondering what to do, a door opened and a waiter came in. He looked just like the one from the earlier cloister who had served us before our departure, or like his twin brother. He was carrying a basket in which there were three apples. He greeted us with a wave of his hand, put the basket on the table, and then left without saying anything. Instinctively, Lui-G took an apple and, pointing to the fruit, he said, "*Some still remain...*" As he said this, we heard his voice amplified, echoing in the great room below. Then Lui-G looked at us and, after a moment, he had a slight smile and said, "*I understand*". And without waiting for us he left hurriedly through the door through which we had entered. We were still hungry. Osc-R and I ate the apples, and then we inspected the scene. The door through which the waiter had entered was locked. After a while we realized we had nothing better to do than to leave the place. To our astonishment, Lui-G was not at the meeting point. Night was falling and as you still had not come, we continued our way until we reached the road. As we walked, a taxi stopped next to us. It was a small van, and there were already three people in it. We boarded, and the taxi dropped us off at the foot of a small building with a digicode. We typed the letters R and S, and upstairs there were two small apartments that seemed to be expecting us."

Lui-G, who seemed to have ended his discussion, saw us and approached with a large smile and open arms.

"Welcome to this place…" he said a little like a host receiving his guests, "I guess you have understood as well, why we are here."

Somewhat taken aback, we did not reply immediately, and he continued without waiting for our answer. "Anyway, tomorrow at the same time, I will explain here what I have found."

Then he waved his hand, and walked away mingling with other passers-by.

We watched Lui-G leaving, and for a short while I had the elusive feeling of seeing a familiar face in the crowd. After a moment of hesitation, we sat around a small free table where a parasol extended its welcoming shade. Without having asked for anything, a young impassive faced woman put four glasses of apple juice on the table and disappeared.

"Do you think he has found the answer?" asked Agn-S

"Who?"

"Lui-G! He told us he knows why we are here." she said.

"Apparently, tomorrow we will have the answer to that burning question," said Osc-R.

I was puzzled, and very eager to know what Lui-G had to say.

24 - TANDEM

Alex arrived five minutes late for lunch.

"Excuse me, usually you do not arrive really ahead of… Well, I mean you're often in a rush…" he stammered aggravating his case.

"Yes," replied Matthew, "but I wanted to make sure we had a private table apart for discussing quietly."

"Since we are not going to discuss work, and you want to be quiet, I can only assume that you have a nice plan to propose. Is it diving or sailing?

"You almost guessed," said Matthew, laughing, "but what if we ordered first before entering the core of the subject?"

For dessert, Alex, completely stunned, was not even thinking about reproaching Matthew for his lie on the reasons for the lunch. He was intensely thinking.

"I do not know whether it is feasible", he said after a moment, "but we will try…"

"Here's how I see it," Matthew said "there will be three projects that will each have to remain separate and independent as long as possible. Officially two of them will be developed to meet the needs of a specific client. The third project is supposed to be an internal project, aimed at improving social relations within our company. It will be our task to refine and adapt the specifications of each project, as and when they progress, and to prepare their future interfacing. Rudy will be in charge of the team that will develop a sophisticated software for knowledge extraction. Chloe will be responsible for developing a multi-agent system. Finally, at some point we will need someone with competencies in group psychology and psychology of individuals.

Alex was more or less expecting what was to come…

"How's your wife?"

He decided not help Matthew.

"She's fine thank you…"

"She is still dealing with psychology?"

Alex, still determined to let Matthew figure it out by himself, replied neutrally, "Yes, she is very perceptive, and she is a woman who knows how to observe situations,"

Matthew took a sip of wine and said, "No, I wanted to ask you if she still practices as a psychologist… I think she would have the expertise and skills to help us… wouldn't she? And maybe she's available…"

"Yes, that is correct, Kristen is a clinical psychologist, and she also has a degree in social psychology… She has taken a year off to know where she stands and to take stock of her situation. But first, I do not know whether she would want to take part in a project, nor whether she would agree to work with us… which means work with me… And I'm not sure I'd be comfortable working with her if I know all the ins and outs of what we want to do, and she only knows part of them. I'll talk to her, but it will surely require some reflection."

"I understand… anyway, to start that phase we have some more time."

When Matthew returned to his office, his computer screensaver was not frozen this time. But at the bottom of the screen of the first moving stylized computer, there was the sequence of ones and zeros which he recognized. Also he could discern on the next screen a similar sequence. Using the recreational properties of the small software, he clicked on the moving computer and, after the zooming effect, the image of the next stylized computer screen took the place of the previous one. It displayed the sequence '00111101'.

It did not take long for Matthew to calculate that this sequence was the number 61 expressed in binary language.

25 - TWINKLES

Laur-N and I decided to continue to visit the place. Late in the afternoon, we arrived near a small hill on the outskirts of the city, which seemed to dominate it. A lane, or rather a small clay road seemed to beckon us to take a walk. We began to climb as the sun was setting. At the top, there was a round stone tower, a dozen meters high, topped by a dome. A few meters away, as an invitation to contemplation, we found a small bench that faced the city. Darkness was coming, and the facades of the small buildings began to light up. We stayed until the night came.

We were lost in silent contemplation of the twinkling lights of the city, when Laur-N remarked, "All these lights are amazing; in fact they do not twinkle, they blink…"

And indeed, as she said this, I realized the incessant ballet of lights that were flickering on and off the facades of the buildings. The moon rose, and we took advantage of the light to go down again. We arrived at what we began to call 'our building' and we each returned to our own apartment.

As I was walking through the rooms, I noticed a detail that I had not yet realized. Every time I entered a room, the light came on, and every time I left the room, it went out. Through the window I could see the facades of nearby buildings; on each floor the lights kept moving. When I was about to fall asleep, those in my apartment went out by themselves…

The next morning, Agn-S, Laur-N and Osc-R, knocked on my door.

"Would you agree to a meeting over breakfast?" asked Agn-S. I let them in and we all sat down.

"Lui-G is not with you?" I asked.

"We assume that he inhabits apartment G; we knocked on "his" door last night and again this morning, but there was no reply…"

Agn-S continued "I do not know what Lui-G has found, but I'm in the dark…"

"So am I" said Laur-N, "and the lights of all these facades flashing on and off at night do not enlighten me," she added, smiling

"Especially since the lights in the rooms of our apartments turn on and off without our needing to intervene," I added.

Osc-R said, "Regarding the buildings, have you noticed that for each building, for each facade, and on each floor, there are nine windows? Eight are equally spaced, and then there is a ninth, a little apart at the end of the row?"

Then changing the subject, he asked, "Do you think the waiter and the waitress, in the cloisters we visited, are the same as those who served us in the cloister where we were prisoners? Or are they look-alikes? And in this case, how many doubles are there?"

"Yesterday, for a brief moment, I thought I saw the face of the waiter in the crowd," I said.

"I think I also saw the waitress on the square in the late afternoon," added Agn-S.

We remained silent for a moment, lost in our thoughts.

Then Laur-N broke the silence, "I do not know why, but I feel that if we can find out why we had a halo over our head, we will have taken a big step in our quest."

Agn-S said, "Finally, except for our group who had halos, for the moment we haven't met anyone from our cloister outside, and maybe the halo was a necessary attribute to be able to get out…"

"And not to disappear… because the threat was clear!" I pointed out.

"If we follow the hypothesis of Agn-S," said Laur-N, "then halos do not mark a physical attribute, since in any case they have now disappeared and nothing else in our appearance seemed to distinguish us from the others."

"Perhaps the halos have been distributed according to a random draw", suggested Osc-R.

"It's not impossible, but in this case what is their relation with the apparent determinism of the events that have led us here?" I replied.

Breakfast dragged on, and the time came when we had to go and listen to what Lui-G had to say.

26 - ADDITIONS

Matthew was tired but he did not want to go home. With a smile, he recalled that he was invited over for a drink with friends committed to 're-socializing' him, but he was not in the mood for that. He did not really feel unhappy, but he was not happy either. For sure, he had the heavy responsibility of a vital and fascinating project, and it stimulated him, but he felt that the way he lived his life was not... harmonious.

His thoughts turned back to Aloïs who was a man he appreciated and respected. Sometimes his speech could seem arid, almost boring, but Aloïs was very gifted for shaking up interesting ideas. Matthew vaguely felt that he could be a source of inspiration. Affection as well as intuition were leading him to spending more time with the old professor. And moreover, with a new set now displayed on his computer, maybe Aloïs would have some more ideas about these irritating sequences of zeros and ones produced by the software he had given to him. But was it quite normal that he preferred to have tea with Aloïs rather than have drinks with friends?

Aloïs always seemed happy to see Matthew who had the rare privilege to be welcome even when unannounced. However, in order to respect the calm necessary for a person of his age, Matthew tried to visit him in the late afternoon or early evening, usually about at the same hours, when his professional obligations allowed it.

Every time he conversed with him, Matthew was intrigued by Aloïs' way of thinking. While preparing tea, Matthew declared, "Last time when I was just about to go, you spoke about an indicator of isomorphism..." and, cowardly hiding behind the understatement, he added, "Well, I'm not sure I have fully understood what you meant."

Outside in a symphony of crackling, hissing and shocks, a crane truck had begun to unload onto the street imposing concrete blocks, probably intended for the process of modifying the next intersection into a roundabout.

After a brief glance out of the window, Aloïs replied, "When I was young I had a math teacher who used to begin his first class with the following proposition, ' Humans are divided into 3 categories: those who can count and those who cannot .'

Then he took five pieces of sugar next to the kettle, and grabbed the magazine on which he had scribbled Newton's formula during Matthew's previous visit. Then he arranged on the magazine three pieces of sugar above the formula, and two below the formula.

"How many pieces are there above the formula?"

"Three…"

"Congratulations! And how many below?"

"Two…" replied Matthew who was beginning to wonder whether Aloïs was taking him for an idiot.

The little game went on.

"Now I will show you how to know how many sugar cubes are on the magazine." Aloïs said.

He gathered all the pieces at the bottom of the page and began to count "one, two, three, four, and five." Matthew thought to himself that if he had not known Aloïs for so long, he would have believed the old man was beginning to lose his mind. The latter continued his lesson.

"Of course, it would have been easier to proceed in this way, and he wrote: '3 + 2 = 5'.

Again, Matthew did not at all understand what his old friend was getting at, but Aloïs continued.

"You could say that by writing out this little addition I have created a picture of my operation on the sugar cubes and I have put it on paper. But it's better than an image…

"Really?"

"Let us suppose that I want to add the five pieces of sugar, that I have just counted, to one hundred thirty-two thousand three hundred forty-three other pieces of sugar stored in a warehouse. If I were to proceed by grouping all pieces of sugar and counting them, the process would be rather difficult and time consuming, if not impossible. It is better to write '132 343 + 5 = 132 348 pieces of sugar.' So my image, not only is the 'picture' of the operation that I could have done to consolidate and recount all these sugar cubes, but it allows me to get the result '*instead*' of this process. I no longer need to handle sugar cubes to know what will happen. Even better, if instead of sugar cubes I need to count concrete blocks which cannot be moved, I can still know the result of the combination of my two stocks of blocks.

In other words, in the world of my written additions, I can simulate and predict what happens in the physical world where I have to handle my sugar cubes and concrete blocks. I suppose all this seems obvious to you, right?"

"Yes… maybe," Matthew replied evasively.

"Between the physical world of my stocks of sugar cubes or concrete blocks and the 'world' of additions of cubes or blocks, there exists what is called an isomorphism. Mathematicians, as usual, define this much more rigorously. But, simply put, we can say we are in the presence of an isomorphism when, for a given operation, one can simulate in a world (that of additions for example), what is happening in another world (that of sugar cubes or concrete blocks, for example), while being certain that the results obtained in either world are always perfectly matched.

To anticipate, act and make decisions, one only needs to use the world in which the manipulation is easiest, or even the only one possible. These two worlds are not identical and, *in a way, one can even say that they have nothing to do with each other.* Yet they have the same structure, and we can consider them equivalent regarding the relationship in question (in our example: adding). We can then choose to operate in the world that suits us best. Thus I can choose to use the world of my additions, rather than putting together concrete blocks and counting them.

The crane truck had finished its noisy operations and was gone.

Matthew was about to ask another question when, much to his surprise, Aloïs looked at his watch and said, "In order to continue this interesting discussion, you will have to come back, because I have to go out…"

"If you have to run an errand, do you want me to accompany you?"

"No, I have an appointment," he said, smiling. Then, pointing through the window to a white Renault stopped at the door of the building, he added, "My usual taxi is expecting me."

Before he left, just in case, Matthew showed Aloïs the new sequence of zeros and ones produced by the screensaver software. Aloïs merely said, "This is the number 61 expressed in binary notation. My version of this software does not produce such things."

Leaving the building, Matthew told the taxi driver that his client was coming, and asked him to wait a little.

"No problem," the driver replied, "I know him well; wherever he goes he uses my taxi, and he is a charming old man."

Matthew smiled, and walked to his car, hoping that the late appointment of Aloïs was not related to a health problem.

The rain had begun to fall, and although he had yet to read a document for the next day, he thought that, after all, he still had time to go have a drink with his friends concerned about his social life. That was when he realized he had left in his office the USB flash drive containing the document that he had to read for the next morning's meeting. After a short hesitation, he returned to his workplace. As he was nearing the office, he had to brake abruptly, bothered by a white taxi coming from the opposite direction trying to avoid a cyclist. 'White seems to have become a fashionable color with the taxis, and even the drivers look alike. Perhaps there are trends with taxis like there are trends in the prêt à porter clothing...' he thought.

27 - SPEECH

The place was still attended by a quiet crowd, apparently indifferent and aimless. But just as before, people were talking in low voices, and the atmosphere did not seem relaxed. Lui-G had climbed on the edge of the fountain, and with a compelling voice he invited people to approach and listen to what he had to say. When a compact and sufficiently large group was formed near him, he made a curious speech.

He began with questions.

"Who among you knows why we are here?"

People did not react; then he formulated the opposite question.

"Who among you does not know why we are here?"

A few hands began to rise in the crowd, followed by others, and after a few moments, it seemed that everyone had raised his or her hand, including us.

"Where were you before you became aware of the world around us? Where do we come from? Where are we going? What are we here to do? And who built this city?"

The crowd did not react.

However a man said, "The buildings, buses, roads, in fact the whole city was built by people who were here before us..."

"Yes, but before them? What was there? It is clear that someone has created all of this... A creator who cares about us, who created our world, and that provides for us... And us... who created us? It had to begin somewhere!" replied Lui-G.

A woman intervened.

"If it had to start somewhere, then there is also a beginning for the creator, so is there also a creator of the creator?

"And in this case", went on a man, "there also needs to be a creator of the creator of the creator, and you can continue to infinity."

Lui-G remained unabashed.

"No, the creator was not created; the creator has always been here…"

The crowd seemed to divide, some approving what Lui-G had said, others siding with the opinion of his opponents. Another woman spoke up.

"If he has no beginning, and has always been here, he has been here for an infinite time…

"Yes, he has," confirmed Lui-G.

"So that means he's been waiting an endless time before creating us and everything around us," and she added, smiling, "one wonders what he was doing for all this endless time before creating us… it must have seemed long to him…"

Without knowing why, I could not help but think that, all in all I still preferred the idea of an infinite iteration of creators of creators, rather than a single creator who had been living for an infinite time in the past and who had done nothing for an eternity.

Lui-G seemed upset; apparently he had convinced only part of the assembly who had been listening to him. The crowd that had formed to hear him dispersed in part, but about twenty people seemed to linger around, showing their approval of what he had said.

We walked around for a while in the square, and from the snippets of conversation that we could hear, we realized that opinions were divided. Then we decided to sit at an outdoor table.

After a moment, Osc-R thought aloud.

"At least it has the merit of simplicity…"

"What are you talking about?" asked Agn-S.

"The explanation of Lui-G…"

"Yes it's true," I said, "but unless you get to meet this famous creator in person, it does not get us very far…"

At this point of our thoughts, Lui-G, who was passing by, saw us and came to sit at the table.

"What do you think of my discoveries?" he said with a smile.

"You mentioned discoveries," said Laur-N, "Tell us what you found and how you have found it," she said in a voice that betrayed anxious curiosity.

"When we visited the cloister with Osc-R and Agn-S, after the waiter gave us apples, I told you, '*Some still remain*' and we all distinctly heard my voice echoing in the dining hall. Then I understood that we were the instrument of a higher power, who instructed us to convey, and implement his will. But I needed to think about it by myself, and I left. I walked on the road for a long time.

Since there is a higher power, able to use us for his purposes, it is clear that it is He who is responsible for us, and for all that happens to us. So He created us, and our purpose is to serve Him.

Then a bus stopped and brought me here."

"But did you meet him?" I asked.

"Who?"

"This higher power…"

"No, or rather yes, I can say that I met Him insofar as I am able to interpret His wishes, from what happens to me and from the world I see around me. Thus one can even say that I meet Him every day…"

"But why doesn't this power come forward directly and explain to us what we are doing here and what he wants?"

"Because it is His will… and I am responsible for enforcing His will among us…" he added with a smile that seemed a little forced.

"How are you sure that you're right?" asked Agn-S.

Lui-G remained silent for a moment in his chair, seeming to reflect, he then replied.

"Because I am totally convinced… because I know… And I'm sure you too will eventually admit His existence and you will serve Him. Then he got up and left the table with a small wave to say goodbye."

We all kept silent for a while, then Osc-R reacted.

"What surprises me is not so much his beliefs - why not after all? - but the limited evidence on which they are based…"

"What I find strange is that he has no real answers when asked why he is so convinced that his explanation is correct," said Agn-S.

"Convictions are a comfortable mattress on which the lazy mind can doze…" murmured Laur-N.

"I think we need to continue seeking out information on our own, and share everything learned to get a clearer picture." concluded Osc-R.

The proposal sounded good, and we agreed to meet again the next day at breakfast to take stock of the situation.

28 - AGENTS

The following day, Matthew invited Chloe to join Alex and him for lunch. They were sitting around the table and she seemed impatient to know more.

"So? Are we going to deal with bees, wasps, or hornets?" she asked.

Creative action caused Chloe intense jubilation; however, she was also a person in whom the cohabitation of rational and emotional thinking was particularly coherent. Thus, without even being aware of it, she gave her interlocutors the pleasant sensation of a young woman driven by intense liveliness and yet great serenity.

"Before addressing the subject," replied Matthew, "can you talk a little more about multi-agent systems?"

Chloe thought for a moment.

"First, I should clarify what is called an agent in this realm. It is an entity, such as a robot or a computer entity with a set of attributes programmed by its designers…

Each agent has a set of 'perceptions'. If it is a robot, perceptions are signals from sensors. If it is a computer entity, perceptions are formed by messages received from a virtual environment, or received from other agents when they are designed to communicate."

The waiter came. She paused to order a duck breast, and after having cleared her throat, she continued.

"Each agent also has a set of 'knowledge' about the nature of its environment, and a set of 'reasoning' rules it can use. It is also equipped with a set of achievable 'actions' such as, move in its environment, send messages, update its knowledge etc. And all this is done according to 'trends' or 'goals' that have been assigned to the agent."

Matthew was captivated, but he could not have explained if it was due to the subject matter or the assertiveness and vitality radiating from such an angelic face. He undertook filling his glass without succeeding in taking his eyes off her. She repressed a smile as he wiped the consequences of this attempt with a paper napkin, and she continued.

"An agent can associate one or more actions from those possible, for each combination of knowledge and perceptions.

It has an evaluation system allowing it to rank such actions by order of efficiency or utility. This allows it to select and take the actions deemed most efficient for the objectives for which it was programmed."

"So we can say that an agent is a real or virtual robot, progressing by itself, in a real or virtual environment." summarized Alex.

"Yes, and to speak in a more familiar language, we can also say that it is a computer entity that has the capacity for autonomy, since it can react without human intervention. It also has the capacity for responsiveness and interaction with its own environment that it can perceive and modify. It has the ability for initiative as well, because it acts according to the trends and goals that have been provided to it. Also we might possibly argue for its sociability, in cases when it can communicate and interact with other agents. Video games often use such systems… But these kinds of systems can also be employed to study group behavior. For example, groups of very simple agents can be used for modeling behaviors of bacteria colonies."

She took a moment to savor her duck breast, and continued.

"Using this method to study social insects requires more complicated environments and colonies of virtual agents. As I said to Matthew when we first met, one can see that it is possible to reproduce the behavior of a real colony by programming agents with elementary behaviors, and without these elementary behaviors having any direct reference to the whole colony's purpose. When observing the colony as a whole, what we call an 'emergent behavior' appears. Everything works as if the colony had a collective intelligence allowing it to ensure its own sustainability, and without any of its agents, being 'aware' of the purpose of the entire colony."

29 - ICE FIELD

Laur-N was strolling through the square, observing people, scanning faces, trying to guess their thoughts through their actions. They looked similar, yet they were all different.

Then an obvious idea popped into her head, so obvious that she wondered why neither she nor her companions had thought about it before.

They needed to know the experiences of the people around them, and for this they would have to try to talk with other persons, rather than only with their cloister companions.

She spotted a young woman sitting at a table on the terrace, in front of a large glass of apple juice. Absorbed in her thoughts, her left hand on the collar of her blouse, she was mechanically rolling something between her fingers and seemed to be watching the people carefully. Without really knowing why, Laur-N felt like approaching her. She sat at a nearby table and was also served a juice. She realized she did not know what to do… The only memory she had of talking to a stranger was also one of her oldest, when she had offered sparkling water to Li-O during the meal she had called 'The original meal.'

The easiest way was to try without ceremony…

"Hello," she said," I'm Laur-N, do you mind talking a little with me?"

The young woman, interrupted her thoughts, shuddered slightly, turned to her and stared at her rather surprised. Then her face relaxed and she smiled faintly.

"What would you like to know, or to tell me?"

"If you do not mind, I'd like to know how you came here."

"Well, I think I'm Soph-E. My earliest memory is quite recent… a week ago... I found myself at a meal, in a sort of cloister governed by strict rules. We could not get out of the cloister and I spent a few days there with other people...

"I see... and after a while you noticed that some of the people had halos over their head..."

"No, I have not seen anyone with a halo... Actually, in the cloister there was a courtyard and the only way out seemed to be a door in the wall surrounding the yard. By going through this door, you could reach the bank of a small lake that surrounded the entire cloister. The water was freezing and there was no boat in sight... At one point, a block of ice appeared, floating near the cloister. The first day I went out several times, and I saw that the ice was growing, almost visibly. In about twelve hours, the block of ice had developed so that it had covered the entire lake."

"So you decided to cross the lake walking on ice in order to see what was on the other side?"

"Yes, but it was not that simple... At first, the door in the courtyard wall was open, and all the cloister's residents were able to see the phenomenon, but no one dared to venture onto the frozen lake. But less than an hour after covering the lake, the ice had completely disappeared. And on the second evening, shortly before sunset, it was no longer possible to get out because the courtyard door was locked. During dinner a voice announced that the surface of the block of ice tripled every hour, and that one solid block would cover the entire lake in twelve hours exactly. The voice added that then, after half an hour, the ice would disappear."

"Did you know whether the phenomenon would start up again?"

That evening no... In my room, I found a message telling me it was dangerous to stay, and that those who could, had to try to leave. There was also a verse mentioning a rope and control of fate by efforts..."

"*Those who, through their efforts, will firmly hold the rope,*
Soon shall master their fate, and be able to cope." Laur-N murmured.

"Exactly," said Soph-E, who did not seem surprised by her intervention.

She continued, "On the third night, at the end of the meal, a voice was heard again, announcing that the ice would begin to reappear in blocks precisely at 10 pm, and that there would be three blocks. Each block would be identical to the one we had seen. Each block would triple its covering area every hour; and a single block had the ability by itself to cover the lake in twelve hours exactly. When each block would have grown sufficiently, so that the three blocks together would cover the entire lake, the ice would remain solid for thirty minutes. The voice added that those who were to leave would have only one chance, and that they should come to the door at the precise hour they had chosen to leave, without warning or talking to anyone."

Laur-N said, "So if I understand, you knew that one block covered the entire lake in 12 hours, and that there would now be three blocks, appearing at 10 pm. The surface tripled every hour, and you could try to access the lake once. Therefore it was necessary to choose the right time."

"Yes, when I reached my room, I thought that I had to leave at night, four hours after the onset of icing, because there were three blocks and one block covered the lake in 12 hours. The prospect of walking on ice at night at 2 a.m. did not please me much. But while I struggled against sleepiness in order not to risk falling asleep and losing track of time, I suddenly realized that my calculation was wrong. I knew with certainty *** what time I had to leave. I fell asleep because I had time… The next morning at nine o'clock I went to the door. We were about a dozen. The door opened, and the lake was completely covered with solid ice…"

*** *The reasoning of Soph-E:*

If a block triples its surface every hour, and alone takes 12 hours to cover the lake, at the 11th hour it will only cover one third of the lake. And if there are three blocks, at the 11th hour each will cover a third of the lake, so all together the three blocks will be covering the lake at the 11th hour.

She continued, "We crossed, and as soon as we moved away from the lake, the temperature became much nicer. We walked on a rather pleasant trail climbing up a hill, and from the top we saw other cloisters…"

"Were they located near a small wood?"

"No, they were much like the one where we were coming from. Each was in the middle of a lake… We had come from one of these cloisters, and we wanted to unravel their mystery. We split into groups, and with two companions we came close to one of them."

The closer we got to the lake, the more the temperature dropped. The lake was free of ice, but a kind of narrow pack ice adhered to the bank. When we approached the edge, there was a crash, and three strictly identical blocks detached from the bank and began to drift towards the cloister. There was no way to get any closer, and we could only turn back... We walked on a road, and a minibus dropped us off at the bottom of a building, where the apartments seemed to expect us.

30 - AUDACITY

For dessert, Chloe chose a raspberry cake. Matthew ordered a chocolate mousse, and Alex had merely an espresso. Then Matthew began to explain what Chloe's project would be.

"One of our clients wishes to study collective behaviors, and has asked us to develop software capable of modeling the evolution of groups of beings. We will have to create a multi-agent system, or a set of multi-agent systems in order to do so."

"What kind of... *beings*"

Alex intervened.

"Well, this is the specificity of the project. It should be adaptable to studying various types of groups, from the simplest to the most complex, say from bacteria to mammals, and insects as well..."

Chloe looked alternately at her two interlocutors, slightly surprised by such a vague request.

"To say the least, neither the individual behavior, nor the environment, nor the type of relationship between individuals, are similar... And what kind of group sizes are we talking about?

"They can range from as few as ten to a few thousand elements," said Alex.

"Or even more." added Matthew.

Although she did not show it, she was very disappointed. She thought that given the positions they held, Matthew and Alex had to be structured and competent persons. Obviously, they were not aware of what they were asking... There was a moment of hesitation, during which Chloe concentrated on the fresh raspberries embedded in her cream cake, Matthew assessed if his chocolate mousse was doughy or creamy, and Alex stirred his coffee.

Matthew broke the silence.

"Our client has requested strict confidentiality, and for the moment, even we ourselves do not know who will be the end user. But the client seems ready to invest heavily in this experimental project. To the extent that our expenses are justified, budget should not be much of a problem."

"It is clear," said Alex, "that a project which is so flexible and versatile, requires that the final product be fully customizable. In short, the type of population studied should not be an integral part of the final product. Rather it should just be a variable input entered into the software, using a set of input parameters according to the needs."

'... *Easier said than done*,' thought Chloe.

Matthew added, "In addition, regarding the computing capacity necessary to run the software, the customer seems to be willing to use the resources available on the market, either directly or through rental. The system must therefore be able to operate on an ordinary computer for simple and small populations, and on larger machines in case of large or sophisticated population modeling."

Alex continued.

"We will need to be able to define the characteristics given to the system's virtual agents, and the characteristics concerning how they interact with one another as well as with their environment. Moreover, we will also need to be able to make the system evolve, and make its characteristics more complex depending on our needs."

As a conclusion he said, "After having studied the problem, we will build a team of analysts and programmers in order to carry out the project."

The alternation of details given by Matthew and Alex, gave Chloe the impression of listening to a play in stereo. 'After all', she thought somewhat reassured, 'they seem to know where they want to go, but that does not mean that it is feasible...'

"So?" asked Matthew, "Do you agree to join us?"

"The project seems very difficult and daring," she replied, "but exciting... and 'nothing ventured, nothing gained'. Of course I will be very happy to be part of it."

However, the explanation about the reason and the purpose of the project had not fully convinced her and, without really knowing why, the story did not seem entirely clear. But she enjoyed the challenge, and the personalities of her two interlocutors pleased her.

"It is a large scale and difficult project," she said. And somewhat provocatively she added, "I hope the stars will come to our aid. What sign are you?..."

Matthew answered first:

"My sign is Taurus, but as is well known, like all Taurus, I do not believe in astrology..."

"As for me," said Alex, "I am Capricorn, but I believe neither in astrology, nor in ghosts... and they do not believe in me..." Chloe smiled and thought that she already fancied working with them...

31 - BRIEFING

The next morning, as agreed, Laur-N, Agn-S and Osc-R, arrived at my apartment for breakfast to take stock of our thoughts. While enjoying a croissant, Osc-R said, " I have carefully watched the lights on the facades... As we have seen, on each facade there are eight windows per floor, plus an additional window, smaller and slightly separated from the others. Apparently, these small windows are not part of the apartments..."

"Maybe they each belong to an equipment room," suggested Agn-S.

"Probably... But I have been observing the lighting sequences of the different groups of windows. For each group, the number of simultaneously lit windows is always even. In other words, if an odd number are lit among the eight windows on a floor, then the ninth smaller window is also turned on. But if, among the eight windows, an even number of them are lit, then the ninth smaller one will remain dark. The lighting of the window groupings is not random... Or at least not entirely... But I do not understand the logic..."

We remained silent, each of us trying to find the meaning of it all.

"If all this has a meaning, we lack the decoder..." sighed Laur-N.

After a moment, as no one responded, Agn-S changed the subject.

"I once again spotted our duo of waiters or their lookalikes... And I followed them. What is striking is that unlike the others, they always seem to be busy. They slip amidst the passersby watching and listening to everything that is said. Sometimes they separate, and I had to choose which one to follow; but it does not last very long, because they eventually meet again."

"Do they look wary, and watch whether they are followed?" asked Laur-N

" No they do not look worried at all. They seem to focus on what they are doing."

" Do they talk?"

" Not much, they seem to tacitly understand each other, and they do not talk to others…"

"Do they have a favorite place?" I asked.

"They are mainly on the square, but they have spent a lot of time at a terrace where Lui-G was sitting accompanied by a man and a woman with whom he seemed to be having a lively discussion. I could not hear what they were saying because all the tables were occupied around them. The pair of waiters were sitting next to Lui-G's table. They were not saying a word… Maybe they listened to the conversation taking place at Lui-G's table… After a moment, still silent, each of them showed to the other a short necklace concealed beneath their clothes.

"Were the two necklaces identical?" asked Osc-R.

" They looked alike; they were both composed of eight pearls, but they were different - Black, Black, White, White, White, White, Black, White, - for one, and - Black, Black, White, Black, White, White, White, White - for the other… After Lui-G left his interlocutors, both waiters stood up and went towards the fountain. For a moment, they looked intensely at the sphere on which the bronze statue sits… Then they seemed to make a final inspection of the square, and left. They headed to the place where the bus dropped us off, and boarded a minibus. The woman was driving, and they took the road by which we arrived here…"

Once again, we were silent, trying to find coherence in all this. But the new information did not provide us the expected enlightenment. Then it was Laur-N's turn to tell us about her encounter with Soph-E. Her narrative really interested us because it showed that, contrary to what we had thought, the process by which we had arrived in the city was not exactly the same for everyone.

"It seems that the thought mechanism dictated in the cloisters, serves as a filter to determine who will get out and who won't." she added.

As for me, before we had this discussion, I had spent time thinking about the problem of the halos.

"Yes," I said, "it is true, and furthermore, every time it seems that the problem is 'complete'; that is to say that, the solution can be found without having to refer to any elements external to the problem. In other words, the problem contains within itself all the elements necessary for its resolution. However, between the problem of the halos and the problem of the ice, there is a slight difference. Without any intervention on our part, our halos seemed to be attributed to some of us and not to others. While in order to cross the lake, what those who wanted to leave had to discover was not an attribute they owned, but an outside phenomenon…"

32 - TRANSMISSION

On Matthew's computer, the screen saver software had continued its whimsical behavior. Three new sets of zeros and ones had appeared and, together with the previous ones, there was a total of five successive moving screens each displaying a sequence of eight binary characters. From time to time the letters A and G also appeared. And every time Matthew saw that the software had produced a new sequence, his association of ideas led him to think about Aloïs.

As a matter of fact, Aloïs had asked him to be kept informed, and Matthew felt like visiting him. However, during his previous visits, Aloïs had simply translated the numbers in the decimal mode and had not seemed to really pay attention to them.

This time was no exception and while, as usual, Matthew prepared their tea Aloïs said, "We have five sequences of binary numbers corresponding to numbers 70, 61, 107, 109, and 77... There are probably more to come."

He stopped talking, and looked at Matthew.

"You look disappointed. I admit that what I just told you doesn't help us a lot. It reminds me of a famous anecdote that one of my professors... of Philosophy...used to tell me, if I remember correctly:

A man asleep on a train awakens with a start, afraid of having missed his station. He asks the person in front of him 'Where are we?' The latter gets lost in a long reflection, and after a moment he says 'In a train...'

The train arrives at the station. The man gets up and, while recovering his suitcase, he says to the person, 'Goodbye Mr. Mathematician.' The latter, taken aback, asks, 'How did you know I was a mathematician?'

'Well, for three reasons: firstly, you thought long and hard before answering, then your answer was perfectly accurate, and finally, your answer is absolutely useless.'"

"I strongly suspect that you did not quite agree with your Philosophy teacher," Matthew hinted.

Aloïs smiled and changed the subject.

"In fact, last time, I did not express myself starting from the right angle. I should have started with the example of another isomorphism, and this one does not directly relate to mathematics.

Considering the existing relationship between thought and language, or more precisely between thought and speech, we could also see it as an isomorphism. This is because an element of the universe of thought can, in principle, be expressed by an element of the universe of speech, and the result of an assembly of thought elements is concordant with the result of the assembly of the corresponding word elements. Conversely, when someone hears words, they are translated into thoughts in his brain…"

"That is a way of seeing things," Matthew replied after a brief moment of reflection, "but one can also believe that thoughts would not exist without words, and presumably words do not exist without thoughts… So have we really got an isomorphism in this instance? Or are the two systems, that of thoughts and that of words, so entangled that they make only one system?"

"It's a broad debate which I believe is not yet resolved," said Aloïs. "It is true that not only can one wonder if thoughts have long existed before words or if the two have developed simultaneously, but one can also question whether they are different systems, because they have such a structuring role for one another. Yet I am inclined to believe that these are two systems both linked by an isomorphism."

Matthew smiled.

"In any case, whether through an isomorphism or not, I suggest we take tea, and I should be able to understand your answer!"

"With pleasure," said Aloïs, "and you're right, this example is perhaps not the most obvious. So let's take another example: speech and writing. We can consider that every word can be written, and that everything written can be transformed into speech… This is a form of isomorphism that seems clear to me… I send you a letter or an email, and when you read them you can almost hear my voice speaking directly into your head. What do you think?"

Matthew remained silent for a while.

"Yes, thoughts can be expressed both in a written system and an oral one. Not only can one make a connection element to element between the concepts expressed in each system, but there is also a correspondence between the results of the manipulations of these concepts produced in each system; and this meets your definition of an isomorphism.

However, you cannot transmit the intonations, emotions, or any other feeling in writing, except imperfectly using additional descriptions or typographical tricks."

"You are right, writing allows only partial and incomplete transmission of speech…"

"Moreover, continued Matthew, the same question about feelings can be asked: if you try to translate feelings into oral or written words, it seems even more incomplete. Indeed, in the field of love, feelings, emotions, the correspondence seems to me hardly accurate."

"Certainly," nodded Aloïs, "however, if we exclude the areas that you just mentioned, regarding the handling of a wide range of other concepts, there exists an isomorphism between written words and speech, even though it is incomplete and some aspects of oral speech are not encompassed. So, if I write you a letter, and for example you read it aloud to one of your friends, the thoughts that arose in my head will be transmitted relatively faithfully to the brain of your friend through the use of two successive isomorphisms…"

They stopped talking, and Matthew began to think that if this conversation on isomorphisms was transcribed and subsequently read by a third party, then its content would reach the brain of that person through an isomorphism. Aloïs had probably followed a similar direction of thinking, and he broke the silence.

"We can transmit to each other our ideas about isomorphisms… Thanks to an isomorphism!"

33 - INVARIANTS

Osc-R and Agn-S had decided to return to the square in order to try to get more information. Laur-N wanted to talk to Soph-E and went looking for her. As for me, I resolved to devote the rest of the day to the 'Invariant-couple'. That was the name I had given in my mind to the pair of servers, who seemed to be a permanent element in the numerous environments we encountered. Given the diversity of the places where they had been seen, once more I wondered if it was a single pair or several perfectly identical couples.

So I walked to the square and sat at a terrace, determined to watch people until I saw my 'Invariants'. The behavior of the crowd had changed imperceptibly. It now seemed less homogeneous and more active. People frequently circulated in small groups and some had lively discussions. The terraces, like the one where I was, were livelier.

I also noticed a surprising novelty. Now there were some men in the crowd wearing ties and a few women were wearing high heels...

After an hour, my wait was rewarded, and I saw a waiter entering the square. I got up and decided to follow him. He walked towards the fountain and its statue, and made his way across the square from side to side. I was following him at a distance, so as not to be seen, but when we left the square, the crowd became less dense, and I had more and more difficulty concealing my surveillance. But the Invariant-waiter was not preoccupied by me. He walked at a steady pace and never looked back. Maybe he did not imagine he could be followed, or perhaps he was completely indifferent. So I relaxed and let myself be dragged into his walk.

Arriving at a crossroads, he met the Invariant-waitress, who seemed to expect him, and they continued their walk together. Soon I realized that they were heading towards the hill where Laur-N and I had climbed together. Gradually, as we approached the foot of the hill, there were other people apparently heading in the same direction. When we arrived at the beginning of the path leading to the top, about forty people were in the shade of the trees. The Invariant couple settled slightly apart under one of them, and I did the same a little further. People were talking quietly, and seemed to be waiting for something or someone.

After a moment, Lui-G arrived, greeted by a murmur of satisfaction, and he climbed on a small rock that was there.

Then a curious scene began.

34 - DECODER

Now Matthew was beginning to understand what Aloïs meant, and he summarized.

"So according to you, there are simple isomorphisms, when they are restricted to one or several operations such as the addition of stocks of sugar cubes or of concrete blocks, as well as much more powerful isomorphisms such as the one between thought and speech, or the one between speech and writing, or the one existing between mathematics and the physical world..."

"Yes... In fact, something extraordinary happened. First, humans discovered the complex isomorphisms between thoughts, spoken, and written language, which is already quite amazing. Then, by identifying other isomorphisms, at the beginning relatively simple ones (such as adding integers, that allowed them to manage and use quantities), then more and more complicated ones (such as the formulation of geometric rules allowing handling shapes in space), they eventually identified complex and very powerful mathematical isomorphisms (such as the one between geometric objects and the real or complex numbers). Meanwhile they realized that the mathematical system that was taking shape, allowed better and better description and prediction of the behavior of nature; hence the reflection of Galilee, later confirmed by the work of Newton and many others, which says that nature expresses itself in mathematical language..."

He took a sip of tea before he continued.

"Mathematics works as a breadcrumb trail, or rather as a rope which leads to treasures unobtainable otherwise... Provided you do not let go of the rope!"

"But do we know why mathematics is the language of nature?"

"No... nobody knows... For about the last four hundred years, everything seems to demonstrate that there exists an isomorphism between the mathematical language created in our primate brain and the physical universe in which we are."

"And of course this has broadened our perspective..." muttered Matthew.

"The isomorphism existing between mathematics and the physical world, gives humans a power of prediction. And it gives them access to things that would have remained otherwise completely inaccessible to them forever. It has made it possible to predict physical phenomena before they are even detectable."

Aloïs was passionate about the subject, and his face took on an almost juvenile expression while he was developing his explanations.

"Among the best known examples are the electromagnetic waves, of which radio waves are a part. Predicted mathematically by Maxwell, they were physically detected by Hertz several years after Maxwell's death. But there are many other examples, such as the discovery of the planet Neptune, and more recently, the discovery of particles like the neutrinos, or the Higgs bosons, discovered years after they were predicted mathematically."

Aloïs' eyes were sparkling; he paused for a moment before concluding.

"The discovery of an isomorphism linking the mathematical system and the physical laws is the best tool for understanding our universe. And today there is almost no action in our daily existence that does not result, directly or indirectly, from the discoveries this has generated. And it has changed our lives... sometimes for the better, but also sometimes for the worse..."

Matthew commented, "So, according to you, spanning generations, mankind gradually creates his cerebral decoder permitting his understanding of the universe in which he lives."

"Yes, in other words, I think we can consider that there is an isomorphism between some creations of human brains, and the universe in which humanity is immersed."

"So this is the reason why you think that human brain interactions reveal isomorphisms and gradually create the decoder which allows them to read the universe?"

"Yes, and I am even tempted to go one step further... Since human brains reveal little by little these isomorphisms, giving access to hidden truths of the universe, so these truths potentially exist (or in a latent state if you prefer) within them. So, perhaps we can consider there to be a latent image of the universe in the human brains which is revealed across generations... And, as I have already told you, I like to think that, through a cooperative networking of brains, humanity continues to decode these isomorphisms. If humanity does not self-destruct beforehand, one day humans will have the answers to the big questions that mankind has always searched for about the universe. They will know how and why the human beings came to be in it..."

He added after a moment, "But maybe these answers will be disappointing for our egos."

The crane truck had not come back to install the concrete blocks stored at the edge of the street. Through the window, they could now see a group of teenagers who were probably returning from a school activity. Some of them jostled laughing, climbed on the blocks; others were more anxious or seemed tired. Aloïs was looking at them pensively.

"It is heartbreaking that, prior to overwhelming them with courses and exercises, we do not explain to our children what it is all for and why studies require a big effort. They should be told that refusing to study math and physics is like refusing to learn how to read and write. They are in fact depriving themselves of the essential tools for understanding the world in which we are. It is like refusing to make the effort to take a difficult path that climbs to the top of a mountain, and accepting never to contemplate the unique panorama which unveils itself once at the top."

As Matthew was about to leave, Aloïs added, "If one day you have children, which I wish for you with all my heart, do not forget to pass on this message when they are old enough..."

"*If I continue to live my life this way, it's not going to happen tomorrow*" thought Matthew.

He took a casual voice and replied.

"There is another version of the math teacher's joke you told me the other day:

'Humans are divided into 2 categories: those who think humans are divided into 2 categories and the others...'."

"I think we understand each other..." Aloïs replied with a smile.

35 - AMBITION

Rudy was perplexed. He had no antipathy for Matthew. Indeed he even found him rather congenial. And when he used to meet him at the informal events inevitably created by the social life of the company, it was not without pleasure. However, recent developments had caused him an unpleasant impression.

There had initially been the meeting during which the Boss outlined the not very rosy prospects. Yet what bothered him most was that, at the end of the meeting, Matthew had been invited to a private interview with the Boss. Then, there was the discussion he had had with Matthew. The project of a 'knowledge extraction' system was interesting, but why had the project been proposed by Matthew, and not directly by the Boss?

Matthew was not his manager and, as a matter of fact, the main motivators in Rudy's professional life were not only compensation, but also the conquest of power. His behavior at work was not unlike Pac-Man, the little character from the 80s video games, whose sole purpose was to devour as many pac-gums as possible, while avoiding ambushes from the ghosts in his environment.

Of course, Rudy had requested a meeting with the Boss to confirm that he should devote his time to this ambitious project, and to determine how often he would have to report to him on the progress of project.

Rudy had received a friendly reception, but contrary to his expectations, the Boss had confirmed that, for this project, Rudy would report to Matthew and not to him. Although he had not perceived any signs indicating a change of his position in the organizational chart from the Boss, nor any intention to make him report to Matthew beyond this particular project, Rudy had come out of the interview with his stomach knotted up by the direction this case had taken. On the one hand, it frustrated his hegemonic instinct; on the other hand, even if his hierarchical position was not threatened at the moment, all this created a precedent that he did not like at all…

He reflected for a while, thought about a certain Justin he knew, and dialed his phone number. The answering machine told him that Justin was not available, so he left a message offering to have dinner with him on the following Monday.

36 - DOCTRINAL PRAYER

The crowd approached the makeshift pedestal, and Lui-G began to interrogate the assembly… or rather, he sort of chanted questions that the assembly seemed to already know. And the assembly answered on the same chanted tone.

Lui-G, "*Is there a creator?*"

Assembly, "*How could we be here, if He did not exist?*"

Lui-G, "*Is He only one, or are there several?*"

Assembly, "*If they were several, who would have made them?*"

Lui-G, "*Is there one Creator?*"

Assembly, "*Yes there is one only, who created Himself*"

Lui-G, "*And what is our role?*"

Assembly, "*Always to be thankful, always to venerate,
Make Him known everywhere, and always do His will*"

Lui-G, "*Pass on such knowledge, and pass on such truth,
With a sign at the feet for her, and a sign at the neck for him.*"

All together: "*MN*"

Contemplating this scene, I mused that Lui-G had really not wasted any time… He got down from the rock on which he had climbed, and the assembly began to disperse. The incantations of Lui-G had created an unpleasant feeling in me, and I thought that I did not want to meet him. So I decided to deflect my attention to the pair of Invariants, but they had already slipped away, and I barely had time to see them disappearing around the corner going up the hill.

I hesitated for a moment, and then decided to climb the hill too. When I reached the top, they were not there. I thought they had gone back down by another road; I looked around but found no one. But as I was about to leave, I heard a noise coming from the tower. I sat slightly apart, and watched. After a few minutes the door opened and the couple of Invariants came out of the tower. They still did not seem to worry about being seen, and I saw them going down the same path by which we had come. After a few minutes, I approached the door of the tower, but it was closed. There was a digicode displaying letters, but all my attempts to unlock it were unsuccessful. I walked away lost in thought while gazing absently at the tip of my shoes slightly veiled by the dust of the road. Then an idea came to my mind, and I turned back in order to spend a few moments with the digicode.

37 - JUSTIN

Justin had accepted Rudy's invitation. Officially, the company for which he worked was a competitor of Rudy's. But actually, it was slightly more complicated.

Indeed, their companies often happened to answer the same calls for bids, target the same clientele, and offer similar services, which led to ruthless struggles between them to appropriate the markets. But sometimes the complexity of certain projects, their scope and risks, led these companies to share the work based on the resources available within each of them. They formed occasional alliances or joint ventures, or sometimes one of the companies would become a subcontractor to the other. And, in such situations, it was necessary to be able to cooperate and join efforts on a project for a common goal. In these cases, one had to collaborate with a company and with the very same people who had been (or still were) an almost implacable enemy on one or several other projects. These alliances of convenience resulted, among those responsible for implementing them, in an attitude slightly tinged with schizophrenia.

Rudy and Justin had studied in the same school. Not being in the same year, they had not specifically hung out together during their studies, but they knew each other. Such situations were not so uncommon in their business community because, once their studies were finished, graduates often targeted the same type of activities, and conversely, a lot of companies were seeking to recruit in the same environments.

They had crossed paths several times during their professional careers, and each had been able to appreciate the skills of the other, sometimes at his own expense. A kind of complicity, had therefore been installed between them, however not devoid of a good deal of suspicion.

Rudy arrived a little early and was soon joined by Justin. He was about the same age as Rudy, slim, with keen eyes topped with a broad forehead enlarged by an early onset of baldness.

The restaurant was famous for its seafood and its cozy atmosphere created by the spacing of the tables, which was favorable for an informal and discreet discussion.

They each ordered a grilled sea bass, and began an overview of their companies' respective situation, the market in general, and their activities in particular. As was customary when they met, each tried to say as little as possible, while obtaining the maximum information from the other. Rudy opened the game.

"So? What are you busy with, these days?"

Justin quoted two or three public calls for tenders, which was not really committing, because they were already known to market participants, since they were public.

"And you?" he continued.

"Pretty much the same things," Rudy answered evasively.

The beginning was laborious… Then, for good measure, Rudy added two items to the list of cited calls for bids, and lied shamelessly mentioning a strong interest of his company for one of them. So having given important information, he hoped to be paid back. Also, if Justin's company was interested in this tender, Rudy could perhaps negotiate the withdrawal of his company against something interesting.

Justin was not duped. He knew too well the business and its environment to be fooled. He concluded that the call for tenders mentioned by Rudy probably did not interest his company. In fact, both of them had much more interest in non-public calls for proposals, restricted to a handful of companies shortlisted on their skills, or even better, in contracts negotiated by mutual agreement with customers running out of time, because these cases were much more suitable to small arrangements between potential suppliers.

There was a moment of silence, during which, for appearances, each of them got dutifully busy extracting the bones of their fish. Rudy did not want to make a stupid move. He brought up the discussion about search engines, their performance and trends. Justin was relaxed, talking about a subject that he deemed riskless, and he was vaguely wondering what Rudy had in mind. On the occasion of a short question, he thought he was beginning to perceive his motivations. Rudy was filling Justin's glass, and talking casually.

"And knowledge extraction? Have you got any interest?"

Justin was taken aback, he knew that his company's research department worked on this subject among others, but he was not aware of any immediate or potential outcomes in the short or medium term which could lead to commercial developments for his company. He decided to avoid the issue and wait for the result.

"You know quite well that we look at everything..." he replied smiling and looking voluntarily without conviction, "Why?..."

Rudy, who was desperately trying to understand where this project, of which he had been given the responsibility, came from, decided to say the least possible to try to know more.

"I understand that some key market players have major projects with rapid developments in this field," he said in a tone of confidence... "Have you heard anything about that?"

Justin, slightly confused, had to admit that, no, he had no specific information on this subject. But perhaps Rudy had made a mistake, because Justin concluded that the company employing Rudy was probably in discussion with a major potential customer on a project of this kind, and that Rudy wanted to know if Justin's company was also working on something similar...

The next day, Justin told his boss that he thought that Rudy's company had probably decided to be active in the realm of knowledge extraction. And his boss seemed extremely interested. As soon as Justin had left his office, his boss called his secretary

"Can you please ask the young Nigel up to see me?" he asked...

38 - PROSELYTISM

Agn-S and Osc-R were sitting at a table and watching the crowd. A man and a woman strolling across the square, headed in their direction. All of the tables around them were occupied, but on the neighboring terrace, some were free. Once close to them, the man and the woman briefly looked around and, addressing them with a smile, asked permission to sit at their table. Agn-S and Osc-R accepted with good grace. The man wore a tie, and the woman had stilettos. Just as she sat, the woman asked, "Do you know Lui-G?"

"Yes, we know him" said Osc-R, slightly surprised by the question.

They seemed amazed at Osc-R's response.

"Ah, you already know him? We have not seen you attending his meetings," said the man.

"What do you think about him? And then, why don't you wear a tie or high heels?" the woman asked.

"Don't you think he's right?" completed the man.

Despite the couple's smiles, Osc-R and Agn-S did not feel very much at ease under this avalanche of questions, and Agn-S decided to try to regain control of the conversation.

"Yes, of course..." she said without elaborating. "But you, yourselves, why do you think he's right?"

The man smiled, slightly condescending, and looking a little like a big brother who would explain life to his younger, he answered as if it were obvious.

"We do not '*believe*' that he is right; we '*know*' he's right."

"And what makes you think that?"

"It is a conviction," he said somewhat haughtily. "It is also called faith... If you are lucky enough to have it, let yourself be guided by it, and you will reach the truth!"

They remained silent for a while,

Then Osc-R asked, "Can you tell us how and for how long you have been here?"

The woman said, "As for me, I was in a kind of mansion, surrounded by a lake. One evening, a voice explained that the lake was freezing periodically…"

Osc-R was about to tell her that he knew the story, but before he could interrupt her, she continued.

"I did not understand what was happening, and when I reached my room I found a note saying that I had to try to leave the mansion. I was tired, and anyway since I did not know what to do, I fell asleep. I woke up a little before nine o'clock, and just in case, I went to the door that led to the lake. A dozen people were there. The door opened, and given the lake was completely frozen we crossed. Then I walked to the road, and a bus brought me here."

"And you?" Osc-R asked, turning to the man with the necktie.

"I too was in a kind of mansion of which no one seemed to know how to get out. In my room, there was a heavy door with a combination lock with three buttons, graduating from zero to nine. Awaking in the morning, I often had the impression of having dreamed of the correct numbers during the night, and I used to test them on the combination lock. One morning, the combination worked… The door opened, I followed the stairs and long corridors, and I found myself outside the mansion. The rest is the same, I walked, and a kind of taxi brought me here."

The woman resumed, "But if you go to the meetings and do not wear ties or high heels, it means that you do not agree with what Lui-G says!"

"To tell the truth," answered Agn-S, "we do not know Lui-G through his meetings, but rather before we arrived here. We know some of his ideas, but from what I understand, we don't know them all…"

"So you really should come to our meetings," said the man, "because Lui-G answers many of the questions you have surely asked yourself."

Osc-R and Agn-S did not really want to prolong the conversation. They took leave, much to the regret of their interlocutors it seemed. But they said they would certainly go to the next meeting organized by Lui-G.

39 - POLYVALENCE

Unlike most of her friends, who had turned the search for a soul mate into an obsession, Chloe did not care too much about her love life. On the one hand, she had a rare ability to find and enjoy the good things in life regardless of circumstances. On the other hand, she had complete confidence in herself, and was convinced that when the time came, she would have no difficulty to recognize and choose the right person. For now, although frequently approached, she was fully satisfied with her cat, the friends with whom she used to socialize, and her work which had taken a new turn and allowed her to reconnect with her previous research.

With Alex' help, she had established a core of competent collaborators, and taken on the task with enthusiasm. She had re-examined her student work, and from there, had gradually complexified the multi-agent system of virtual bees that she had established a few years earlier during her doctorate.

Obviously, because of her company's power as well as its technical, human, and financial support, the job was taken to a different scale, and the developments were much faster than when working on her thesis. However, the goal too was on a much larger scale, and she was not even sure it was achievable.

"The versatility of the system is essential," Matthew reminded her at a meeting.

"Yes," Alex added, "we need to model various kinds of groups of entities, and this is a major challenge of this project."

"Well," Chloe said, "the team has begun to compile a list of 'libraries' to make the system configurable." When she spoke about her work outside of her team, she preferred to use a common language, rather than the more precise (but more arid) vocabulary in use in information science such as ontology, objects, classes, etc.

Alex had a slight smile, Matthew relaxed and Chloe continued.

"There will be a 'library of environments'; that is a list and description of the attributes of each of the environments in which the virtual agents may have to operate. And since we spoke of mammals as well, it will be possible to define the characteristics and attributes of various land environments, such as savannah or jungle. Thus, once the agents' characteristics have been defined, it will be possible to choose the virtual environment in which they may operate.

"Will it be possible to change the characteristics of an environment, if necessary?" asked Matthew.

"Yes, we hope to do so", she said, "and because the library is not exhaustive, we will also be able to add new environments if required, provided they are correctly described."

She continued, "Similarly, we will build a 'library' of possible interactions between the agents and their various possible environments."

"And these interactions will also be configurable, right?" asked Matthew.

"Yes, not only the interactions with each environment will be defined on request, but the cognitive and logical abilities of the agents will also be chosen in a logical and cognitive profile 'library'."

"Will it be possible to change these profiles, or add new ones if necessary?" Matthew asked again.

Chloe felt a little embarrassed. From the first time Matthew and Alex had described the project to her, she had the feeling that she had not been told everything. This impression had persisted over time, and Matthew's questions reinforced this feeling.

In response, she slightly smiled and nodded.

"And regarding the interactions between the agents themselves?" Alex asked, more in order to inform Matthew than for himself.

"There will also be a 'library' of interactions and possible modes of transmission of knowledge between agents, with profiles ranging from non-communication to complete communication of each agent's knowledge to the others (or some others), and with or without distortions."

Then, without waiting for Matthew's question, she looked at him with a twinkle in her eyes.

"And I believe we will have to ensure that the profiles communication can be configured or new ones added, if required..."

40 - LOOP

It was early afternoon, and we were all meeting at Laur-N's place to assess the situation. She had joined Soph-E and had invited her. We would have liked to invite Lui-G to join us, but we did not have the opportunity to meet him since the time he had exposed his theories to us.

Agn-S and Osc-R talked about their curious conversation with the couple wearing a tie and high heels. Likewise I described my surveillance of the two Invariants, Lui-G's curious diatribe at the foot of the hill, as well as my visit to the tower located at the top of the hill.

"We should try again to speak to Lui-G and if we cannot, at least attend one of his meetings in order to try to understand," Agn-S said.

"And as for me, I'd like to know what is in that tower," whispered Laur-N.

Then, after a moment of silence, Osc-R tried to sum up things.

"Last time, Laur-N said she thought that both in our cloister and in that of Soph-E, solving riddles was a kind of filter in order to determine which ones could come out. Li-O noticed that, in both cases, the riddle contained, within itself, all of the elements needed to solve it. Shortly before, Agn-S said that she thought the halo we wore in our cloister seemed to be a necessary attribute allowing us to get out... I think we should continue to explore these ideas..."

"Things are not that clear," I said, "the conversation Agn-S and you have had with the couple with the tie and heels, seems to show that it was also possible to escape some cloisters by chance..."

"Yes, it's true," Osc-R said, "we will have to also clarify this aspect, but I feel that we must first focus on what has enabled to get us out..."

I felt he was right.

"In fact, concerning the halos," said Agn-S, "there are two ways of looking at them… We can consider that it was just a distinctive sign and that the opportunity was given to those who were lucky to have it, to earn their freedom by solving the riddle. In this case who distributed the halos? Why us? By chance? But perhaps there was a second level… I have wondered if the sign did not only constitute a distinctive sign, but also indicated that those who were lucky enough to have it, also possessed within themselves the tools necessary to get out of the cloister where they were locked up."

"What do you mean by tools?" asked Soph-E who had remained silent until then.

"Well, suppose for example, that the halo signaled those who had the curiosity in themselves to go outside, or those who had in them the need to break free of the obstacles they do not understand…"

Laur-N nodded.

"In other words, if I take your first example, those who were curious enough to be willing to leave, would have been provided with a halo, or conversely, those with a halo would have been equipped with a strong curiosity, driving them to leave…"

At this point I thought a clarification was necessary.

"The idea is interesting, but we must not forget that we received a chilling warning i.e. those with halos had to leave the cloister under penalty of 'disappearing'… Therefore, curiosity or desires for freedom were not necessary to motivate us…"

There was a long silence during which everyone was absorbed in his or her thought. After a while Laur-N recited:

"Those who, through their efforts, will firmly hold the rope,
Soon shall master their fate, and be able to cope."

Then she continued.

"This could be interpreted as an encouragement to voluntarily use a method and stick to it. The reward for such use would then be mastery of our destiny… Now suppose that the tool of which Agn-S spoke consisted of the knowledge and control of deductive and inductive reasoning and that, in our cloister, the halo was the hallmark of those who had the chance of having such a tool in themselves… It seems to me that this could enlighten many things…"

Laur-N's surprising proposal immersed us again into deep reflection and perplexity. The hypothesis was worth examining.

Soph-E broke the silence.

"You mean that, in your cloister, the halo would be the interpretation, in the visible world, of the ability of some people to make logical inferences, and that it would have hence designated those of you who were lucky enough to have this ability?..."

After a pause, she added , "But in this case the system loops..."

"Yes, admitted Laur-N, "we come to a 'self-reference' because if the halo is given to those who have the capacity to reason and thus solve the puzzle..."

Agn-S completed "...this means that it is their ability to perceive that they have a halo which confers a halo to those who have it.... Indeed, as Soph-E said, it loops... In this particular case, the string of logic seems insecure... And yet..."

"And yet," I pursued, "we know well within ourselves that in the world in which we live... whatever the logical system, there are statements from this system for which it is impossible to say whether they are true or false..."

"Yes," said Osc-R, "we know it as if it was engraved in us... A kind of 'incompleteness theorem...' How have we learned that? I guess like me, you do not know..."

Soph-E summed up.

"Our self-referential loop can be summarized as follows: the logical tool, interpreted in the visible world by means of a halo, was given to those with the rigor of reasoning necessary to find out that they had a logical tool.

She paused then wondered out loud.

"Could it be that Laur-N's statement is part of the 'undecidable' statements of 'our' logical system?"

"After all," I said a moment later, "the only thing that matters is whether Laur-N's assumption allows us better understanding where we come from and better predict where we are going. According to this hypothesis, and as suggested by Agn-S, if we went out of our cloister, it is because 'we only' had the chance to have the tool to get out. And if we had not had this tool, we would not be here to ask the question..."

I felt there were other things that did not work with this explanation; and my concerns probably bothered my companions as well...

41 - KNOWLEDGE

Rudy had also started working, and although he had no specific experience in the field of knowledge extraction, he was used to project management, and had the necessary skill set to organize a team of specialists and have them work together.

Instinctively, the complicity that seemed to have developed between Matthew and Alex displeased him. Yet he knew that Alex of course, as an engineering manager, had to be involved in the technical guidance and orientations of the company.

Initially, with Theresa, he had examined the profiles of the company's employees most likely to possess the expertise and skills necessary for his 'knowledge extraction project'.

He had realized that the Management was very interested in the project, not only because they had not opposed any internal staff transfers implied by the project, but moreover because they had even favored them.

Then he had asked Theresa to hire a high level expert in the field of knowledge extraction. They had chosen Theo, an academic about forty years old, specialist in this field, who, being tired of the successive restrictions on budgets for public research, was eager to raise his standard of living, and had decided to join a private company.

In order to help Theo devote all his energy to the project, they had decided to also hire an assistant who would accompany him. Someone who would not only be able to work in this realm, but would also be responsible for facilitating his transition to private sector uses. Among several candidates, Theresa had preselected Nigel. He was available immediately and seemed to have all the required skills. She had submitted his profile to Rudy and Alex.

Looking at his CV, Rudy had noticed that he worked for the same company as Justin. He had contacted the latter, just in case, to find out whether he knew him.

"You know," Justin said, "we are several hundred in our company and I do not know everyone."

Nigel had explained that, above all he wanted to work on 'knowledge extraction', and that, in the company where he presently worked, the outlook in this realm and career opportunities for him were not very exciting.

Sitting with Matthew and Alex in the latter's office, Rudy was summarizing the situation, and not without a hint of frustration as usual.

"The team has been assembled. Theo, the senior specialist, and Nigel the assistant that we have hired, seem to be happy; the chemistry looks good since the team quickly set to work." he said with satisfaction.

He still believed that he had not been given all the ins and outs of the project, so he launched a trial balloon:

"Where will the questions come from? And how will they be formulated?"

"You want to know who will issue the search queries addressed to the knowledge extraction system, and how they will be formatted. Is that right?" Alex asked.

Rudy nodded.

"Requests could come from individuals, in natural language…" began Matthew,

"…But they could also come from other programs and in a structured way," Alex completed.

"It does not help me much for the moment…" mumbled Rudy.

"Of course this will have to be clarified in due course," Matthew said in a conciliatory tone.

Rudy made an effort to smile, and when leaving the meeting, he decided that, what they wanted to hide, he would discover by himself…

42 - GLIMMER

It was Osc-R who formulated the problem.

"Independently of the 'self referent loop', and although we all have the intuition, I think, that our hypothesis of a halo as ' an image of a logical tool', may contain part of the explanation, there are at least two very concrete aspects with which it does not fit…"

He continued after a short pause.

"Before we had to leave the cloister, each of us found in his room a note on which the following statement was written: '*All guests in this place reason in the same way.*'

And this information was essential in the reasoning that allowed us to infer that we had a halo. If the others had no halo, then according to our hypothesis, they did not have the logical tool needed to solve the problem. Consequently they would not have been able to reason in the same way as we did, and in such case the whole argument, which allowed us to know that we had a halo, collapses…"

"Osc-R is right," said Laur-N, "and my hypothesis about the meaning of the halo does not hold. We must find another explanation…"

Agn-S replied, "Still, the motto…
'*Those who, through their efforts, will firmly hold the rope,*
Soon shall master their fate, and be able to cope.'…"

This motto was written on every page of the book in our cloister, and also written on tree trunks when we arrived here; it was also indicated in the cloister of Soph-E; and it was the message that we found in the room where we felt free to speak for the first time:

'*You have held the rope and the control of your own fate begins with your freedom of speech.*'

All this seems to indicate that the rope designates logical reasoning, and seem to encourage us to never deviate from it. We, the halo holders of the cloister, have the common characteristic of having kept holding this rope."

Again there was a pause. And after a moment I had the feeling of perhaps glimpsing a glimmer.

"In essence, the important thing was not that the other reasoned really in the same as we did; the important thing was that we *thought* they were reasoning like us. And the function of the message was to make us believe this…"

"In this case," completed Laur-N, "the others have probably not received any message saying that everyone reasoned the same way, and having no means to solve the conundrum, they have had no alternative other than to wait and see… And it becomes compatible with our hypothesis"

After a while, Soph-E noted, "Apparently in my cloister the rope was there, but there were no halos… Maybe there was no visible interpretation of the logical tool in this cloister or perhaps, its display not being essential to go out, I just have not seen it…"

Then she turned to Osc-R .

"You spoke about two aspects that did not seem consistent with our theory. What is this second aspect?

"The second aspect, which our theory does not seem to accommodate properly, is called Lui-G… He had a halo, he came out of the cloister by applying the same logic as we did. But does he hold the same rope as we do? Or has he changed for another one?"

"Maybe he has succeeded in demonstrating the existence of a Creator with the logical tool." Laur-N said softly.

"Whatever his reasons we've got to talk to him concluded Agn-S."

43 - COMPLEXIFICATION

Chloe was progressing. She had asked her team to retain the methods that had been successful for her academic work. Starting from simple situations that she tested and, once successfully checked, she moved to increasingly complex situations that she tested again at every step. Since the system was intended to be used for studying all kinds of communities, from insects to mammals, she began with the former. These were simpler to model, and she knew she would have to progress by successive complexification in order to model other communities.

As planned from the beginning, the team had tried to incorporate some versatility into the system. They had started to create simple virtual agents, whose characteristics were easily modifiable, and put them in simplified virtual environments which were also modifiable. They included a few dozen agents in a closed environment with strictly defined rules. And once the interactions of these agents in this environment had been tested, the situation was made more complex by opening up the environment and allowing coming and going or external influences.

"For now," Chloe explained to Matthew and Alex, "we have created a model that simulates the behavior of fifty bees in their hive without outside influence, but if we change the software's setting parameters, the system simulates the behavior of fifty ants in their nest."

"Does it work well?" asked Matthew.

"It seems to work pretty well, provided that, for the comparison, we can get an idea of the actual behavior of a beehive or an anthill reduced to fifty individuals... and currently without a queen..."

"And it is easily possible to significantly increase the number of agents, isn't it?" asked Alex.

"Yes, the easiest way I have found is to create several small groups of similar agents, and make these groups interact with each other."

She glanced at both of them, one after the other.

"We will now open our beehives or ant nests to the outside, we will introduce queens, but you need to define the priorities. Which environment do we choose first… ants on the ground or bees in the three dimensions?

Matthew thought for a while and looked at Chloe.

"Can you wait for the answer until tomorrow?"

She smiled.

"It should be possible…"

When they left Chloe's office, Matthew asked Alex.

"Is Kristen still willing to work with us?"

"Yes, she has not changed her mind…"

"And…She knows that she will not 'know everything'?"

"That bothers her less than me… But knowing my wife, I doubt that she will remain for long unaware of what we are trying to do."

"I think we will need her to join us within the next two weeks."

"Yes it should be the right time… And for tomorrow, how do we proceed?"

"Well, let's get going…" said Matthew.

44 - GATHERINGS

Lui-G's speeches were no longer held in the central square. Rather than have random people make up an audience, he probably preferred to speak to people who had taken the extra step to come and listen. He now held his speeches under the trees, at the foot of the hill. It was very easy to attend these meetings because you only had to ask a man with a tie or a woman with stilettos, to be immediately informed of the next meeting. These had indeed become almost daily. We arrived a little late, and what looked like a ceremony had already begun. There were about a hundred people. Lui-G sported a large red tie and was perched on a pedestal, which seemed to have been especially brought for this purpose, and a psalm exchange was just ending.

Lui-G: *"Without our obedience…"*

Congregation: *"For us there is no chance"*

Lui-G: *"If with Him we agree…"*

Congregation *"Rewarded will we be…"*

Lui-G: *"MN"*

The structure of the meeting was an alternation of incantatory dialogue between Lui-G and the assembly, and of explanations about the significance of these dialogues. The logic of Lui-G's theory was pretty straightforward and easy to understand. It could be summarized in seven items, plus one:

- Individually we cannot understand how or why we are here.

- Our environment and interactions are coherent, and no one is here by chance.

- Our own complexity, as well as that of our environment, show that there must be an architect: The Architect Grandiose.

- To master this complexity, this architect must be almighty.

- Since he is almighty, the Architect Grandiose presides over all of our destinies.

- We are here thanks to him; so he is generous with us.

- Therefore, we must obey him if we want to continue benefiting from his generosity in the future and avoid incurring his punishment by opposing his will.

Finally, Lui-G was the Mediator Nominated by Him in order to help us understand all of this.

We wanted to talk to Lui-G, after the ceremony, and we attempted to approach him. A lot of people were around him, and many of them wore a tie and high heels. However, when he saw us, he made his way toward us, smiling.

"So?" he said, "what do you think about this?"

Osc-R replied.

"It's very interesting, but there are many things we would like to clarify with you, and it's hard to talk about them here…"

I suggested that we meet at my place, and to our surprise, after a short hesitation, Lui-G agreed.

A few hours later, we were all in my apartment, except for Soph-E who had thought that, not knowing her, Lui-G would speak more easily in her absence.

It was Laur-N who opened the discussion by a seemingly innocuous question:

"Do you know why there are more and more men who wear a tie now and women in high-heel shoes in the streets, and why so many of them attend your meetings?"

Lui-G was relaxed, and he replied immediately.

"Of course I do, I was the one who asked them to do so…"

Then he continued

"I asked those who believe in my ideas and who want to spread them to dress that way. This allows them to recognize each other and to distinguish those who are convinced from those who need to be convinced…"

"But why try to convince?" asked Agn-S.

"When one has understood something, it is natural to be willing to share it…" he replied, a haughty half smile on his face.

"Don't you think that the foundations of your theory are a little 'thin'?" Laur-N intervened.

"It is a matter of conviction, and I know…" Lui-G replied curtly.

"That's what troubles us. Until we joined you here, we had seen a lot of rigor in your deductions…" I said.

Lui-G did not answer, and Osc-R, who had not intervened until now, decided to ask a blunt question.

45 - ANTHROPIC

The following day Chloe, Matthew and Alex gathered in the latter's office

"So? We begin with ants or bees?" Chloe asked.

After some hesitation, Matthew answered.

"As a matter of fact, the aim of our client is to be able to study the behavior emerging from a community of agents with individual capacities for logical inferences."

"Ants and bees... rational?"

"No, no. In fact, neither of them..."

Chloe was only half surprised.

"So we worked for nothing!" she could not help saying.

"But the system you have developed with your team is largely customizable and versatile, isn't it?" Alex intervened.

Chloe nodded and Alex continued.

"It seems to me that what has been done until now makes it possible to envisage a small community of rational agents, operating in a minimalist environment, endowed with capabilities to react and interact."

Chloe had suspected for some time that she had not been privy to all the facets of the project. She decided to find out, in an indirect way.

"But then... insects, mammals... different environments to be defined, savanna, jungle... So what remains from everything we had talked about?"

"Eventually, we will have to deal with that as well, because the aim is to study all types of communities," said Matthew.

"But for the moment, we are not there yet, and we must be more specific..." Alex added.

Chloe saw they both looked uncomfortable, and she insisted in a keen tone.

"But we have to define the type of agents that must have these inference capabilities. You want pseudo cells, pseudo-insect, pseudo-animals, pure logical entities or what else?"

Matthew and Alex were increasingly embarrassed.

"You have to give the system's agents anthropic characteristics, and on this basis, the system must remain flexible and scalable.

"In short, you primarily want a multi-agent system whose agents, immersed in a simple environment, will have to behave like humans endowed with only rational responses. Am I right?"

"Yes," said Matthew.

Chloe was thinking rapidly. It was clear that Matthew and Alex were well aware that a community with only such characteristics did not exist in reality, and that, contrary to what had been the case with ants and bees, there would be no subsequent comparison between the multi-agent system and reality. She concluded that they were not really interested in the simulating specific groups, but rather in studying the overall logic that would emerge from the interaction of several rational agents.

The atmosphere was heavy. She got up, walked to the door and, instead of leaving, she turned to them.

"Why didn't you explain this from the beginning?"

Matthew seemed relieved by the question, but before he answered, Alex replied with another question.

"It has not caused you to waste any time, has it?"

Chloe thought for a moment.

"No, not really... it was first necessary to build the team, then to resume my doctoral work and to think about the foundations and tools needed to develop a complexifiable multi-agent system. But it is time that we know where we are going."

Then, looking into her eyes, Matthew answered her question.

"It's not that we did not want to tell you all the 'ins and outs' of the project, but we could not... I hope you are not upset."

She held his gaze, or rather she accepted his gaze.

"I think you would like to, but you still cannot 'tell me everything'. For the moment at least, we can continue..."

After a pause she smiled.

"No I do not blame you."

46 - REVERSAL

"You really believe the ideas that you profess? Or do you have an interest in propagating them?" asked Osc-R looking straight into Lui-G's eyes.

The latter, while trying to sustain Osc-R's gaze, attempted a biased answer.

"Of course, by definition I have a great interest in what's interesting... and which is true..." This evasive reply left us perplexed and silent.

After a moment, Agn-S continued quietly.

"And you also really believe that if there is an Architect Grandiose, his main concern is to let people find out whether he exists or not, reward those who believe in him, and to punish those who don't? Maybe there are better occupations than this one, no?"

Lui-G fidgeted in his chair and reacted vigorously.

"Have you, yourself, found out what we're doing here? Have you got an explanation? Have you noticed that we are getting more and more numerous, and that if some, like us, arrived after solving a logical problem, there are many who arrived here by chance? Did you notice that since I have spread my ideas, the atmosphere is lighter and that people communicate more because they have a topic to discuss, and they have joint activities? You criticize what I profess, but you have no explanation to offer instead... My explanation, at least, has the merit of existing..."

"Perhaps it would be better to keep searching, rather than just accepting a ready-made explanation," I hazarded, "that would be another way to encourage people to communicate..."

Lui-G reflected a moment, then, seeming to take a decision, his voice became calm and he spoke as if confidentially.

"Suppose that, as people become more and more numerous,

problems arise in the distribution of goods that our environment provides us for the time being. Presumably this will generate conflicts between individuals or groups of individuals. It would be better to be amongst those who decide than to be amongst those who endure... It's a matter of survival... The system that I propose has the immense advantage of sorting out the parties. Those who *do not* believe in my ideas just need to side with me and help me spread these ideas among those who are willing to believe in them..."

We stood a moment stunned by this sudden reversal of perspective.

"So you don't really believe in the ideas that you profess..." Laur-N whispered.

Lui-G replied with a quip.

"In your opinion, on what side am I? That of those who want to decide or on the other side? The answer should give you an idea... And besides, does it matter?"

"How will you distinguish those who have decided to side with you by calculation, from those who really believe in your ideas?" asked Osc-R.

"Again, I don't think it matters much, because what really matters is the efficiency of those who spread these ideas.

However, if I may judge by the number of men who, at my instigation, agree to wear around their neck an attire that requires them to keep their shirt collar closed, thus preventing air circulation inside their shirts even when it is very hot, and if I may judge as well by the number of women who, in order to show that they believe in my ideas, accept not to be able to walk normally and to risk twisting their ankle at any time, I'm not worried about the number of people who will want to spread the good word..."

"You must be hot too..." Agn-S said, pointing to Lui-G's red tie.

The slight haughty smile reappeared on his face and he replied:

"We need to set a good example..."

Then Laur-N asked a disconcerting question.

"Doesn't your pearl necklace bother you underneath your tie?"

For a brief moment Lui-G looked surprised. He took out of his pocket a necklace with white and black pearls, and placed it on the table.

"So you have one too... I thought I was the only one... The clasp is complicated, and I could not remove it before having access to a mirror...

We all watched the necklace for a while ; starting from the clasp, pearl colors were distributed as follows: Black, White, Black, Black, Black, White, White, Black.

Lui-G continued.

"I have not met anyone else with this kind of necklace. For me it's a sign... As soon as I felt its presence around my neck, I knew it was the sign of a Force, and that I attracted power the same way as power attracted me..."

After what he had just confided to us, it was difficult to know whether Lui-G believed what he was saying or whether he was faking it.

"Those of us who had a halo also have a collar. Let us join our efforts and we will be invincible..." he said

There was a moment of silence.

"And if we do not side with you?" I asked.

Lui-G began to fidget again in his chair, without looking at us.

"In this case, I ask you not to meddle with that..." he said in a strained voice.

"Why wouldn't we participate in the debate in order to bring out our own ideas?" insisted Laur-N.

Lui-G abruptly stood up out of his chair, walked to the front door, half opened it, and turned back to us.

"I do not think you quite understand... and I will be clearer... Those who are not with us, are against us." he said in a brittle voice.

Then he went out and closed the door abruptly.

"How did you know he had a necklace?" Osc-R asked to Laur-N.

"I did not know, but I happened to notice that several of us had one. I thought that maybe we all wear a necklace... at least in our group. So, I tried..."

"Moreover, as I could see it, there are at least two collars outside our group; these are those worn by the pair of Invariants. It might be interesting to remove our necklaces and compare them." suggested Agn-S.

Indeed, it was a good idea...

47 - INTELLIGENCE

Because his inclinations were far more political than technical, Rudy completely relied on Theo and Nigel. He believed that once the right team had assembled, his main role was to ensure and facilitate the smooth running of the project, and above all, not to be bypassed as the main interlocutor of Matthew and Alex on one side, and of the team on the other side. His role was facilitated by the fact that Theo and Nigel, having been hired specifically for the project, were new to the company.

Obviously, with Theo, Theresa had found the right man. And Nigel seemed keen to integrate into his new job as quickly as possible. While assisting Theo, Nigel seemed to bear a great interest in all areas of the company's activity. Rudy had approached him, not only for this reason, but also because he hoped to obtain some useful information about Nigel's former employer.

The knowledge extraction software project was progressing well. It was now at the stage of the 'alpha release'; this meaning in the jargon that a version of the software could be run internally, but that it did not yet have all the planned features.

Rudy thought that, objectively, things were not going too badly for him. Still he remained deeply dissatisfied by his dependence on Matthew. Moreover, he had a hunch that, with the blessing of the Boss, Matthew and Alex had not told him everything. In addition, the company's Security Department had implemented incredible procedures to prevent leakage, and they had made sure that neither Rudy, nor any member of his team could have access to the full source code. This general distrust deeply irritated him.

He had realized that Matthew and Alex also headed up a bizarre project concerning bees, which similarly was subjected to the same stringent safety procedures. Knowing that these exceptional security measures were not only meant for his team or him was reassuring, but it reinforced his disgruntlement of not being 'in the big league'.

Seizing the opportunity of a retirement drink, he managed to engage Chloe in conversation. After some small talk and the usual jokes about retirement and their time left before giving their own farewell drink, Rudy started to question her.

"Are you happy with your work? I heard that you were dealing with a new kind of project."

"Yes, and yourself?" Chloe replied, without fully answering the question.

"Well," he said, "for me too, things are going well. I am dealing with a knowledge extraction project, and it's starting to progress. I have been told you were working on insects, and I must say that this is the first time I have heard about such a topic in our company."

Rudy found Chloe quite attractive, yet her reserved attitude annoyed him a little. But he had some understanding of psychology, and this made him all the more dangerous given that he shamelessly used these skills for his own ambitions.

So he continued.

"After all, it is not so much the nature of the project that matters, but rather the feeling of achievement one can get from it. Don't you agree?"

"That is true. Exciting work is not really work... and opportunities opened by knowledge extraction must be captivating." she said.

"But you really take care of insects?" he insisted innocently.

Rudy looked pleasant. Yet, even if the latest developments of the project would, sooner or later, end up being known within their company, Chloe stuck to the original version, especially since Matthew and Alex had asked her to maintain the secret as long as possible.

"Yes, it concerns bees..."

"And who is the customer?" Rudy questioned.

"I don't know... Perhaps an organization which studies beekeeping..."

Their conversation was interrupted by the guests gathering around the future retiree, who was opening his gift. Chloe managed to slip away at the end of the speech, which annoyed Rudy. But finally he was rather happy. She was really very nice. He had broken the ice and if he could combine business with pleasure...

As for Chloe, she thought that Rudy, on closer acquaintance, was quite pleasant.

The following day, Rudy suggested to Nigel to informally meet Chloe's team members and get to know them, in order to further his integration into the company. Rudy's request was less than necessary given that Nigel had already begun to do so.

48 - SLIDE

The temperamental software had finally produced three new series of zeros and ones, followed by the letters A and G which appeared for a short while. Then, nothing else happened. Matthew could have forgotten about all this, because technical support had found no malfunction in his computer, nor in those of his colleagues. However, every time the screensaver software was on, it reminded him of the series of zeroes and ones by posting the sets of eight characters previously produced on each of the first eight displayed screens. All series began with zeroes, and if they were translated into decimal numbers, the following list was obtained: 70, 61, 107, 109, 77, 47, 100, and 50. Aloïs, so far, had not done much to help him with this issue which, after all, was not very important. Yet, Matthew wanted to show him the new list, as he had requested.

In addition, Matthew had often reflected about his most recent talks with Aloïs. Something intrigued him, and it was not unrelated to his project.

There was a park not far from Aloïs' home, where he used to take walks. They had agreed to meet there late in the afternoon. When Matthew arrived, Aloïs was sitting on a bench, a satchel at his side, absorbed in reading a scientific journal. Not far from the bench, there was a respectable size sandbox, with a slide in the center. Some kids were playing under the watchful eyes of their parents. Matthew sat down next to Aloïs. Judging by the grin that lit up his face, he was glad to see him.

He cast a quick glance at the list that Matthew showed him.

"Well, I don't think the list will lengthen anymore."

"So you know what it means?"

"It requires thinking... You see, we have associated decimal numbers corresponding with the binary numbers, but maybe there is another correspondence which could be associated with these binary numbers, and this would give a meaning to this list..."

Then he stopped talking. And since he did not seem to be willing to add anything, Matthew changed the subject.

"Basically, one can speak of isomorphism, when a model can simulate something, and it works particularly well..."

Aloïs thought for a moment.

"I do not think it's only reduced to that ... Assume that you want to build a bridge. Of course, you can make a model, and if it is a particularly suitable one, you can use it to predict the behavior of the bridge in the wind for example, or during an earthquake, or under the effect of an overload. You build this model to simulate the behavior of the structure that will be built.

In my view an isomorphism is not built. Rather it is discovered. An identity of structure and behavior is found between sets (one could say worlds) that, a priori, have nothing to do with each other, but are, nonetheless, in some ways equivalent.

It is not common to highlight an isomorphism. This requires the pooling of knowledge and the efforts of people with exceptional abilities, often during several generations."

Matthew was not totally convinced. He insisted.

"But can one say that mathematics was 'discovered', and that it existed before mankind? Or did mankind build it? In the same way, language and writing have been built and not discovered."

"This is another extensive debate, and again, I do not know if it will ever be resolved. With regards to mathematics, the proponents of mathematical Platonism think, as Plato believed, that mathematical objects exist by themselves, independently. Others believe that mathematical objects are a construction of the human mind. Regarding language and thought, certainly they are linked to beings that think and express themselves, but we can also wonder whether the 'potentiality' to think and express is necessarily linked to the particular species that thinks or expresses."

"The line between isomorphism and modeling is perhaps blurred..." Matthew resumed.

While speaking, Aloïs was closely watching the actions of a little boy in the sandbox. He had painfully climbed the few steps of the slide, and sitting atop he was about to let himself go. Before his mother had time to approach, he had slid down the slope. As he was neither used to it, nor had he the necessary reflexes, he finished the slide a little abruptly, his buttock meeting the hardness of the sandbox. He remained one second aback. Then as if in spite of himself, his lower lip came forward, and while holding his buttock, he walked crying to his mother. Not far away, his little sister, apparently indifferent to all his trouble, plunged her hands, and even her forearms, with delight into the sand.

"Yes, perhaps the boundary is fuzzier than I myself can imagine… This may be a granularity issue," said Aloïs fixing the sandbox.

"Granularity?"

49 - VISION

We had compared the necklaces worn by each of us. They were all composed of eight white or black pearls, each beginning with a black pearl from the clasp; but all the set-ups were different. And they differed as well from the arrangement of Lui-G's necklace and those of the Invariants that Kar-N had described. Surprisingly, even if they all looked alike, we had no trouble remembering the composition of each necklace. It was as if this world of black and white was familiar to us. My necklace was composed as follows: black, white, black, black, white, white, black, white; and that of Laur-N was black, white, white, black, white, white, black, white. With the necklaces of the Invariants and Lui-G's one, they formed a set of seven different necklaces.

I had planned to wait a little, but not too long before returning to the tower, and I proposed to Laur-N to accompany me in the late afternoon.
In order to reach the path to the hill, we first had to go through the square. The more we walked, the more we saw ties and high heels... We were approached several times by friendly couples, who explained to us all the good that Architect Grandiose, AG (so they said colloquially, to show their closeness to Him), wanted for us, and why we should attend Lui-G's meetings. We quickly realized that the most effective way to shorten these forced conversations was to look very interested and ask when and where the next meeting would take place.
When we passed near the fountain, Laur-N stopped, and taking me by the arm, she pointed to the large sphere on which the statue was sitting. Along the equator of the sphere, the eight series of small black and white tiles, looked similar to eight small caterpillars one behind the other. On seven of them, we recognized the same black and white set-ups as on our necklaces...

The top of the hill was deserted. The sun had not yet set and lit up the door of the tower entrance. I approached the door's digicode, and examined it carefully, first from the front and on each side, then from above and below

"What did you expect?" asked Laur-N, with a small smirk.

"Last time, I replied, I tried to put a thin layer of dust on the keys of the digital code, and now I try to see if, some of them were pressed since."

"Even if you succeed, it won't give you the solution…"

The keys of the digicode were labeled with letters, apparently without any meaning or specific order. My meticulous examination showed that the dust was gone on four of them: C, H, S, U.

"If the code has only four letters, then we probably have the solution," I answered, "because in such case, none of them is pressed twice, and, after all, the number of possibilities is not that high." ***

*** -If the code has only 4 letters, and 4 different buttons were pressed, so all the code letters are different.

-There are four possible ways to choose the first letter of the code from C, H, S, U; for each of these ways there are then three possible ways to choose the second letter, which makes 4 X 3 or 12 ways to choose the first two letters. For each way to choose the first two letters, there are only two ways to choose the third, which makes therefore 24 opportunities to select the first three letters. And of course, for each way to choose the first three letters then there is only one possibility left for the fourth letter, which therefore results from the choice of the first three.

Thus, assuming that it was a four-letter code, there were a maximum of 24 possible combinations to try.

Laur-N, who had immediately understood, took a wooden stick, and drew a letter on the ground.

"Let's start with the letter 'C'," she said…. On the seventeenth combination, the door opened.

We entered the tower, and we climbed the fifty steps of a spiral staircase. At the top of the tower, the staircase led to a small circular room with a three hundred and sixty degree outside panorama. We could see the last bends of the winding uphill path from the city. At the center of the room, there was a kind of desk with two joysticks, beside which there were two pairs of glasses. The slight humming of a fan formed a discreet background sound.

After having observed for a moment the landscape and the emerging ballet of the city lights, without even consulting each other, we tried the glasses. They were completely opaque. Each was connected to a wire and a socket, and we realized that the wire end sockets were not connected to anything. While I was trying to find a plug, Laur-N interrupted me, and pointed outwards in the direction of the path. At dusk we could still distinguish two silhouettes heading to the top of the hill.

We put the glasses back in their original position, and we went down the spiral staircase two steps at a time. As soon as we were out of the tower we hid in the bushes, just in time to see, silent as usual, the couple of Invariants emerging from the last bend and enter the tower.

We waited until the night was quite dark, and we went down discreetly to the city.

50 - ENTROPY

For a while Matthew thought that the old man had forgotten what he was talking about, but he went on.

"Yes, granularity is probably the word that best expresses that the scale under consideration influences the perception of modeling. For the buttock of that little boy who just went down the slide, sand can be described as a continuous medium, solid and capable of withstanding a shock, as he just experienced the hard way. And if later he becomes a civil engineer, he will find in the literature numerous equations describing the behavior of this medium. On the contrary, if his sister later decides to make hourglasses for example, she will deem that sand is a discontinuous medium, penetrable, and being able to flow. This will not at all be the same description nor will the same equations apply."

"So we are rather dealing with 'modelizations' which are established according to needs."

The mother of the two young children had pulled out of her bag a plastic bottle half-filled with what seemed to be a mixture of water and grenadine. Then, after giving each of them a drink, she walked to a garbage bag provided in the park, and discarded the empty bottle.

"One can view it this way...," said Aloïs, while contemplating the scene. "But sometimes the distinction is not so easily made."

He leaned over with amazing flexibility, picked up a small stone at his feet and threw it a few meters ahead. Then he went on.

"In the same way as Mr. Newton's equations make it possible to describe the trajectory of a stone and predict where it will fall, one might want to describe the behavior of the air in the bottle discarded by this lady. For this, one could try to write the equations of each air molecule's motion, based on its interactions with the other molecules. Then, if the system's initial conditions are known exactly and if the equations for each of the molecules are correct, we will have a real isomorphism, i.e. a perfect match between the behavior of gases and what is predicted by the equations.

The only problem is that, for the air in this bottle, we will have to solve the equations of about 50,000 billions of billions molecules."

"That's a lot indeed, and of course, for now, with presently known technologies, no computer has such processing capabilities…"

"And we are likely to wait for a very long time… Because, suppose that we could build a machine solving the equations of a million molecules per second, it would take our machine a billion years to process all of the gas molecules contained in this single bottle."

"It's fortunate that she has not thrown out an empty magnum of champagne…" Matthew muttered.

" Certainly, because assuming that despite the complexity of each equation, our machine keeps the same pace, it would then take about 4 billion years which is roughly the age of our planet… and 15 billion years, which is slightly more than the estimated age of our universe, for a jerrycan of air." he added.

"Okay, so no isomorphism for gases…" said Matthew, who suspected what would follow.

"This is not that simple… As you well know, we can still predict the behavior of a gas; even if we cannot solve the equations governing the behavior of all these molecules.

In fact, on our scale, if we know the pressure, the volume, and the temperature of a gas, one can predict its behavior thanks to the laws linking these parameters which were first identified experimentally. And when the gas is not dense, these laws are particularly simple!

Later, these experimental laws were confirmed by a theory based on a purely statistical way of estimating the velocity of the molecules of these gases. Certainly the tiny gas behavioral fluctuations are not taken into account in this description…"

"But that does not bother us because such fluctuations are not noticeable on our scale." Matthew continued.

"That's it! But despite the apparent simplicity of these laws, and their purely statistical interpretation, this model gave rise to extremely subtle reasoning, whose developments helped explain fundamental phenomena in very different fields, such as, among others, why once the mother of these two children has mixed the water and grenadine in the bottle, as long as she might wait, the water and grenadine will never separate again into two distinct parts. More generally it also explains the irreversibility of the evolution of our universe, in which time flows from the past to the future and not the other way around..."

Matthew nodded, and Aloïs continued.

"As a matter of fact, it seems as if particles don't care about the orientation of time."

"You mean that particles are indifferent to the passing of time?"

"No, time matters for them, but the direction in which time flows (i.e. from the past to the future or the reverse) does not seem to matter. In other words, if we could film a particle, and we could then watch the film, there would be no way to discern whether we run the film forwards or backwards."

"However, in the universe we live in, we can clearly distinguish the direction of time that elapses from the past to the future..."

"Yes, but this happens on another level... Let me clarify:

If we trap a '*red gas*' and a '*white gas*' in a box, separated by a barrier, and then we remove the barrier between them, the two gases will eventually mix because their molecules agitate and collide.

Indeed, the gases mix because there are an immeasurably greater number of possible positions for the molecules corresponding to the '*mixed gas*' circumstances, than the number of possible positions corresponding to a '*separated gas*' situation. The same would happen with the children's grenadine and water... To figure it out with an image, there are a gigantic number of possible ways to assemble the various parts of a plane without any order, while there is only one way to assemble them in order that they form a plane."

Matthew, who remembered his courses, completed.

"Yes, although this is theoretically possible, we will never see the mixture of the two gases or the mixture of water and grenadine spontaneously separate again, because in order for the mixture's components to spontaneously separate, there must be a combination of very exceptional and totally unlikely circumstances causing the molecules of each category to collide in a very specific way. And the probability of this combination of circumstances is just infinitesimal..."

"Thus, there is an orientation, a direction in which systems left to themselves naturally evolve towards greater homogeneity. This is called the increase of entropy, and it determines the direction of the evolution of these systems. And if that is so with the systems composing the universe, then this is also the reason for the direction in which things evolve and the reason for the orientation of the '*arrow of time*'."

Aloïs added, half nostalgic, and half mocking, "Besides, I am, as well as you are, one of those systems subjected to the arrow of time…"

He seemed to get lost in his thoughts for a while.

"Aging is not very pleasant," he said "but the alternative is even less encouraging!"

Then, he smiled again, and he exclaimed, "Ah! I forgot… I have a present for you! I found it in an antique shop."

He opened his briefcase and pulled out a small bronze statuette, which he gave to Matthew. It represented a young scantily clad woman sitting on a sphere, holding a tablet in her left hand and whose right hand was positioned at shoulder height.

Matthew smiled happily. One day he had mentioned to Aloïs that he happened to pass by the square of the town hall of Paris, just for the pleasure of contemplating this statue of Jules Blanchard. It seemed to him that the mixture of determination and sensuality emanating from the sculpture, as well as its allegorical meaning, appealed to both his heart and his reason. Aloïs not only had a good memory, but he also was a caring man!

I am deeply moved. She will stay on my desk. Now I will work under her friendly supervision and she will make me think of you!

While he was returning home, Matthew, very touched and happy with his gift from Aloïs, reflected on the conversation they just had. Certainly, towards the end, it had evolved into considerations that seemed interesting, but quite distant from his project. However the first part of the conversation reinforced his feeling that his project could be at best a 'rather crude modelization'. In the end, he had not learned much more about his irritating list of zeros and ones, except that, according to Aloïs, the list was probably now complete. It was certainly unimportant, but he nevertheless decided to email the list of binary numbers, as well as their decimal number translation, to Alex and Chloe, and ask them whether they could see any significance in it.

51 - ALPHA RELEASE

The day Alex entered Matthew's office and, with bright eyes, let him know that an alpha version of the knowledge extraction software was available, Matthew felt his heart beat faster in his chest. They both knew that they were now addressing a crucial stage of their project.

Alex summarized.

"The software seems to produce satisfactory results. If we formulate a question as a query, it searches the Internet and selects all information available on the network concerning the subject regardless of its format. It then evaluates the relevance of the information by comparing it to the information already gathered, as well as evaluating the reliability of the explored sites. It then creates a summary table that includes the logical and semantic links with neighboring concepts."

"Is it already operational?" asked Matthew.

"We cannot yet question it in natural language and queries still must be established according to a specific format. Similarly, the response format is also specific.

"If they worked so far according to our instructions, this should not hinder us…"

"Yes, they have followed the formats that we have specified for both queries and answers."

"And is Chloe progressing with her rational agents?"

"She has made a prototype, with fifty agents in a rather austere environment, but at the moment it is somewhat disappointing because there's not much happening. No emergent behavior has been detected in this community that remains rather passive…"

Before Matthew asked a question, Alex continued.

"According to what we stipulated, Chloe has endowed each agent with the ability to issue queries as soon as they are needed, and to integrate the received answers, provided they are in the same format predefined for the knowledge extraction system. Until now, this ability could not be tested, since the knowledge extraction software was not yet available.

"Well I can't wait to see the result." muttered Matthew.

He took out his phone and asked Chloe whether she was available. She quickly joined them.

"Can you please describe the environment in which your 'prototype agents' are now placed?" asked Matthew.

"For the moment it's a pretty stripped environment, and the agents have knowledge of primary level."

"That is to say?"

"Well, before we talk about their environment, perhaps it is appropriate to clarify the characteristics of the agents. As per your request, they are equipped with logical capacities. This was relatively easy because, for over a century, modern logic (also called mathematical logic), can be expressed using symbols which can be handled by software.

In accordance with your specifications, I have subjected the agents to constraints akin to those of the real world; hence they know they need to drink, eat, sleep, etc. at regular intervals. As such, they have first level knowledge of the environment and of the objects that allow them to meet these needs. They know, for example, how a glass is made up, and that it can be filled or emptied... And the same goes for everything that surrounds them: walls, doors, etc. But, apart from the closed world in which I have placed them, they know nothing yet"

Then Alex showed Chloe how to use the alpha version of the knowledge extraction software.

When she had been asked to provide her agents with capacities to issue queries and to receive information in a specific format, Chloe had immediately understood that her system was meant to be interfaced with a data or knowledge mining software. Not only was she not surprised, but she also felt right away very excited to see the effects of this interconnection with her multi-agent system software.

Chloe was about to leave Matthew's office.

"By the way", she said, "I received your email, but these numbers evoke nothing to me, except eight numbers expressed in the binary system and apparently randomly drawn. What about you Alex?"

"For the time being, I have not found anything..." he replied.

"In any case, this is not essential; perhaps it actually is a sequence of random numbers…" Matthew said.

In order to more easily track the behavior of some of the system agents, Chloe wanted to assign some kind of ID number to some of them. And because these numbers were to be used only as labels, she did not want any apparent relationship among them. The eight numbers sent to her in Matthew's email seemed to do the trick. Back in her office, she hesitated for a moment and, a little for fun, she decided to assign each of these eight numbers to label eight specific agents in the system.

52 - KRISTEN

The official reason for Kristen joining the company was a mission of psychological auditing. She had accepted Matthew's proposal transmitted by her husband Alex. Therefore, there was no need for Theresa to start looking for a psychologist and despite her curiosity she had not asked any questions. Theresa just did her best to facilitate Kristen's integration, since that seemed to be what the management wanted.

Kristen was about thirty-five years old; she was blond, with a slender and sporty look.

A paradoxical mixture of warmth and reserve emanated from her. This gave to those around her the impression of benevolent availability and distance at the same time. She liked Matthew, whom she already knew through Alex, and she immediately got along very well with Chloe.

Initially, Rudy was quite suspicious. He wondered why Kristen had been hired, and was not at all convinced by her audit mission. Moreover, he had discovered that she spent a lot of time with Matthew and Alex.

However, his suspicions somewhat faded when she came to speak with him, along with each of the team members about their working conditions; even more so when he learned that she was Alex's wife and already knew Matthew.

Meanwhile, Chloe was morose. Her project seemed blocked and, as pleasant as the presence of Kristen might be, she did not think she could be helpful.

Sitting in a small meeting room with Matthew, Alex, and Kristen, she reported on the first results of interconnecting the knowledge extraction system with the multi-agent system.

"We have fifty agents in a closed environment, endowed with logic. They have permanent access to a huge knowledge base, which automatically gives them the concepts they need in order to evolve... and nothing happens..."

"What do you mean by 'nothing happens'?" asked Alex.

"Well one can check the records of each agent's actions with respect to their environment or to other agents. Everyone seems to go about their mundane occupations related to their environment, and without much interaction with others. It seems that the queries automatically sent to the knowledge base only relate to identification or use of objects within their reach. The system seems to be in an almost stationary state, and of course there are no emergent behaviors."

They all pondered in silence for a long moment, then Kristen intervened.

"In my opinion, they lack at least two things... among many others..."

Three sets of intensely interrogating eyes scrutinized her, while she continued.

"First they need sustainability..."

"That is to say?" asked Matthew.

"I think they must have a strong tendency to preserve their 'existence'. In other words, you need to set them up so that they foremost favor actions that prevent them from disappearing."

Chloe looked skeptical.

"They do not risk much in their present environment, and I do not see what it would change..."

"This is why we must have a second strong trend," Kristen said, "Curiosity."

"This is a broad concept..." Matthew sighed.

Yet, Kristen remained unabashed.

"Curiosity is one of the most powerful action drivers... We must provide them with curiosity at three levels, by order of importance: with respect to themselves, to others, and to their environment."

A smile began to light up Chloe's face.

"I think I see what you have in mind, she said, and I think you're right. We will explore this..."

Then after a moment of reflection, she added.

"But, if the agents are endowed with these three levels of curiosity, perhaps they will end up raising questions about the system to which they belong, and they might discover some emergent characteristics of their own system... In which case, this could have interesting implications..."

53 - INVITATION

Rudy's project continued to progress at a steady pace, and he acknowledged that Theo was particularly competent in his field. However, this did not make him inclined to feel any admiration nor any sympathy towards him. Indeed, Theo's remarkable intellectual abilities were associated with a rather introverted hardworking and conscientious nature. Rudy felt condescending toward people who did not seem interested in power, money, or political games. On the contrary, he was more inclined to favor the nosy curiosity of the young Nigel. The latter perfectly fulfilled his role of assistant, being in charge of all administrative and reporting tasks, as well as of relationship with the rest of the team. Nigel's hiring permitted Theo to focus on the expected developments.

The team was now addressing interrogation of the knowledge extraction system in natural language. But Rudy found that, curiously, this phase seemed to generate less interest from Matthew and Alex than the previous one. As he was considering this question, Justin called.

"It's been quite some time since we have met. How about a dinner at the same fish restaurant as last time?" he said.

"Why not? Have you got something to tell me?"

"You know we always have things to discuss," Justin replied mockingly. "Tomorrow night. Is it all right with you?"

Rudy thought for a while, pretended to consult his agenda, and accepted the invitation.

The next day Rudy arrived at the restaurant which was fully booked. Justin was not there, and no table had been reserved under the name of either of them. For a moment he wondered whether he had misunderstood the invitation from Justin but, upon reflection, he soon realized that this was not the case. He thought his time was precious and he hated getting stood up. As he was about to leave in a very bad mood, Justin arrived, a little out of breath.

"Excuse me for this slight delay, he said, believe it or not, I completely forgot to book the table, and when I remembered to do so, it was too late. I propose that we take my car, and we go to a restaurant brasserie I know, not very far from here. And they make great sauerkraut."

"Okay. Anyway we have no choice…" Rudy laconically replied.

He had nothing particular against sauerkraut, but he liked to be in control of the situation, and did not appreciate when something unexpected came up… especially when he was not the cause. Once in the car, the moody atmosphere was still noticeable.

Justin tried to break the silence and lighten the mood.

"So? Are you happy with Nigel, your new recruit?"

Rudy was surprised at the question; more by its form than its substance.

"I thought you did not know him… When I asked you, you said that there were hundreds of people working in your company, and you cannot know everyone of them…"

Justin hesitated a little.

"Since you had previously mentioned him to me, I wondered whether he was doing the job…"

Rudy found it surprising that Justin spoke about a person he did not know, and even designated him by his first name.

"Yes, he does his job nicely; he is inquisitive and very effective…"

They were now seated at a table in the brasserie, and Rudy wondered whether Justin had sought to see him for a specific reason. He mused that after all he was not the initiator of this diner, and only had to relax, and wait and see; so, that's what he did.

Instead of trying to get information from the other, as they both used to do, Justin directed the conversation to the vision they each had of their work, their satisfactions, frustrations, stress, and the relative merits of their respective employers.

In his professional activity Justin was not naive. He knew that, even if they were imbued with a real or apparent cordiality, the ties created within a company the size of his employer's, were ultimately reduced to a multitude of 'give and take transactions'. His employer and his colleagues needed his skills and his work for theirs, and he needed them for his work and thus making a living. He was well aware that, if by any chance, it became necessary to reduce costs, or redirect the activities of the company, they would not hesitate to part with him in the least expensive terms. And in such a situation, even if some empathy would certainly be noticeable among his spared close collaborators, they would not hesitate to accept the new policy and even implement it. Besides, what else could they do?

Nonetheless, the many years of his team efforts and work for his company's welfare and survival did not leave him indifferent. The long-standing ties that bound him to the company and his colleagues, as well as the need for consistency and continuity in what was being built day after day, made him feel a kind of loyalty vis-à-vis his company. And it would have taken an exceptional circumstance, or rather a sharp deterioration in his business environment for him to leave.

Rudy, on his side, believed that companies in general, and his in particular, were only seeking condottieri in order to accomplish the tasks they needed. So he clearly regarded himself as a mercenary at the service of those who would maximize his satisfaction in terms of power and money.

Although they were not his, Justin was not surprised by the opinions that Rudy professed on this matter. He was not shocked either; 'after all,' he thought, 'this is perhaps the best way to protect oneself from the economic uncertainties and maintain the flexibility required from employees.' He thought it was now time to reveal the reason for their meeting to Rudy.

54 - SQUARED POINT

Chloe's team had worked feverishly in order to endow the community of agents with the trends suggested by Kristen. But after the excitement of the early days, morale had quickly dropped to the lowest level. Again, in the presence of Kristen, Chloe was summarizing the status of her work for Matthew and Alex.

"Actually, we have noted some increase in the number of requests to the knowledge base, but that does not seem to influence the agents' overall behavior, and there is still little activity."

Matthew was perplexed, and Alex turned to Kristen.

"Do you think your recommendations were not good, or that they were insufficient?"

Kristen looked at her husband, leaned back in her chair, closed her eyes a few seconds and replied.

"Maybe both... Probably insufficient... but on second thought, the lack of results is not that surprising. We may have been a little hasty in our conclusions."

Clearly, since their last meeting, she had continued to think about the problem, and she seemed to expect more or less what Chloe was relating. She continued.

"In fact, the two trends we have introduced are somewhat antagonistic... If the preservation of their existence is a major trend for the agents, they will not take the risk to satisfy their curiosity. And in these conditions, they will not seek to broaden their horizons."

"So we should delete the 'instinct for self-preservation' they have been given, and only keep curiosity?" asked Matthew.

"I don't think so," said Kristen, "without tendencies for self-protection, if our groups of agents become active, they could be decimated."

"We should therefore find a way to oblige the agents to satisfy their tendency for curiosity, despite their 'instinct for self-preservation'." said Matthew.

"Maybe we could even arrange for their preservation instinct to strengthen their desire to satisfy their curiosity," Alex added.

They all reflected intensely and, after a moment, Chloe relaxed, and a half-smile appeared on her face.

"I think I have a lead... I will use a squared point..."

"What do you mean by 'squared point'?" asked Kristen.

"Nothing... it's just a bilingual pun." she said. And she refused to say more, until she had pursued the matter.

55 - PRESSURE

We had agreed to meet Agn-S and Osc-R in the late morning at one of the terraces of the square to decide our future investigations; and Soph-E was to join us. The weather was fine and the temperature pleasant; however, the more we approached the square, the more the atmosphere became oppressive. Eyes down, people seemed to hasten their pace toward their goals, with the exception of the men with ties and women wearing high heels who, whenever we encountered them, seemed to take their time to stare at us insistently and look us up and down. When we reached the square, to our surprise, all the terraces were empty. We sat at one of them where we had agreed to meet the others. We were determined to wait for them. No sooner were we settled, when a man with a tie and a woman with high heels came to our table

"What are you doing here?" they asked abruptly.

"Well we are expecting others…" I answered a little surprised.

"They won't come…"

The conversation was not pleasant. Without being openly hostile, they were insistent, standing near our table, which forced us to look up to speak to them.

"Why won't they?" Laur-N asked quietly.

"Because they've got to listen to Lui-G at his meeting at the foot of the hill…

"They've got to…?" I asked.

"Yes, it's better for everyone… Besides, you also should go."

The tone was firm, but not really threatening.

"Well, we thank you for your invitation, but we prefer to stay here and wait for the people we want to meet…" said Laur-N.

Given that they did not seem to go away, I continued.

"See you soon… maybe we'll see again at the next meeting…"

But they had no intention to move.

"You must go; we must all go to Lui-G's meetings…"

"But why?" I asked.

"It is A G's will, the Architect Grandiose, and Lui-G is his Mediator Nominated."

To signify that our conversation was over, Jessi- K turned to me, changing the subject.

"It's strange," she said, "not only are the terraces empty, but it looks like there is nobody to serve drinks…"

Before I said anything, the man with the tie answered.

"They do not serve during the Lui-G's meetings."

"That's new… has someone decided so?" I asked.

"We convinced them…" the man said, smiling.

He added, "In any case, there is no one to serve you because they are all at Lui-G's meeting… So come with us!"

The conversation was going nowhere; despite the discomfort of the situation, neither Laur-N nor I were planning to move. They insisted, still somewhat authoritarian, but nonetheless polite.

Laur-N ventured a desperate attempt.

"We will not go…, but if you yourselves wish to attend the meeting, you'd better go now."

The woman with high heels took the man by the arm.

"She's right… Come on…" she said

Without adding a word, they turned their backs on us and walked away. As soon as they disappeared, a young woman came and put two glasses of apple juice on our table, then vanished.

Although we did not know how long it would last, we decided to stay until the meeting was over and people came back to the square. After all, the weather was nice and we had something to drink.

56 - SIMULATION

Chloe was struggling to hide her excitement while exposing the recent results of her work to Matthew, Alex, and Kristen.

"Primarily, we had to prevent the system from immediately taking an equilibrium configuration and stabilizing without any further changes. Therefore, we had to avoid making a set of agents each with same skills and behavior."

She paused and resumed.

"I was inspired by a riddle about monks who cannot speak, which some people attribute to the scientist Henri Poincaré. And since we are interested (at least that's what I have understood) in the overall logic emerging from the interactions between rational agents, here is how we have proceeded thus far: we have formed several communities of about fifty agents endowed with curiosity. We have given them as well, to a greater or lesser extent, logical skills, and we have created a strong incentive for them to escape the confinements of their community. We have also established a mechanism, a kind of domino effect, whereby the curiosity of those who have managed to get out promotes the exit of agents from other communities."

Kristen and Alex were taking notes. Matthew, leaning on the back of his chair, was intensely staring at Chloe who continued.

"Into the system we have inserted agents who are not influenced by the evolution of the community. They remain identical to themselves, but their role is both to facilitate interaction mechanisms, and provide a summary of the system status. We have also ensured that most of the agents with sufficient logical skills and curiosity about the outside world can succeed in getting out, thanks to their logical abilities; some others can escape by chance. Finally, we have arranged for everybody to converge in a city. Eventually, all this constitutes a grouping of various logical skills."

"And how does it evolve?" asked Matthew.

"Well, now we have a community of agents in the city that continues to grow. The agents appear perfectly comfortable with the particulars of their environment, due to the knowledge with which they have been originally endowed, and their ability to enrich it resulting from interfacing with the knowledge base. Indeed, it provides them with the necessary concepts whenever they need them."

Chloe respected the moment of silence during which her interlocutors reflected on her explanations. Then she asked the question she had been wondering about for many weeks.

"Adapting environments as well as the number and attributes of the agents, should enable this system to simulate many types of problems for which a formal resolution would be too complicated. So what kind of problems are you trying to address with this project? Optimization problems?..."

Seeming to seek the best way to present their views, Alex and Matthew did not answer right away. Then Matthew spoke.

"Solving problems using the logic that emerges from the interaction of several rational agents is a possible and interesting application of the system we want to develop... But this is only part of what we want to do. Indeed, it is now time to tell you the goal that we were initially assigned at the start of this project..."

Kristen looked at Alex and Matthew.

"I think I understand..." she murmured.

"The aim is to go much further! We are seeking to develop a simulator of human conduct..."

Alex and Matthew just nodded as a confirmation.

Chloe reacted vigorously.

"That's impossible; human behavior cannot be reduced to simple logical reasoning and access to a knowledge base. Our system overlooks a multitude of factors just as important or even more important and which are not quantifiable: emotions, feelings, love, anxiety, etc. How would you introduce them into the system? This has nothing to do with the general tendencies and goals that we have assigned to agents. It's far more complicated!"

"I think that's where I come in…" Kristen murmured, seeming not to believe what she was saying.

57 - HEADING CHANGE

Rudy had accepted the offer made by Justin at the restaurant.

After all, if the company where Justin was working managed to take control of the one currently employing him, it was better to be on the side of the predators than being on the prey side, and consequently be among those who decide rather than those who suffer.

The plan was simple: at best, it consisted in preventing or hindering any major development likely to improve the income of the coveted company whose shares were already rather low. Or at least, to keep the potential predator informed of the targeted company's development plans, in order to allow it to react timely in terms of technical and business strategies. One could thus expect that stock prices would continue to fall, until the predator would strike through a takeover bid.

It would certainly affect the situation of many of his present colleagues, but "well..." he thought, "That's life... there are those who are lucky and those who aren't... those who know how to seize opportunities and those who don't... those who know how to get by and those who get lost..."

Finally Rudy had succeeded, without much effort, in getting rid of what some might have called 'scruples'. The idea that, if all this worked, he would have the opportunity to play a greater role in the new entity, filled him with energy and it made him forget the frustrations of recent months.

Justin had told him that Nigel had been sent 'undercover' to work in the targeted company, and Rudy had requested that Nigel not be made aware of Rudy's new role. In accordance with his natural inclination, Rudy found it more comfortable pulling the strings anonymously. Also, this had the immense advantage of protecting him from an inadvertent gaffe from Nigel. Finally, in case things did not turn out as expected, it would still leave him a chance to stay in his current company if he so wished. All in all, he found the situation interesting... and almost comfortable.

Given the new situation created by Justin's offer, Rudy could not simply wait passively for information to reach him through chance or through informants. He would have liked to take advantage of the widespread bug which activated computer webcams at untimely moments. But according to the specialized press and to his company's own IT security service, this bug only affected the webcams on/off systems, and no files or information were created or sent when this happened.

He had also envisaged hacking into his colleagues' computers or phones, but not having the necessary skills, it would have required accomplices. In addition, the company's security systems, already sophisticated in normal times, seemed to have been strengthened for the project he was interested in. So he opted for a more outdated method, but that technological developments made relatively easy to implement. There was a multitude of commercially available miniaturized gadgets to spy on what is being said in a room. Most of his colleagues usually locked their offices only in the evening at their time of departure. During the day it would be relatively easy for him, under any pretext, to enter their offices in their absence, and stick a mini microphone under a table or under a shelf...

58 - ANALYSIS

Being aware of the complexity of the project and the need to progress in its realization, Kristen and Chloe used to prolong their discussions and reflection in the office, well beyond working hours.

"From the middle of the twentieth century," said Kristen, "much work has been undertaken in order to try to describe the elements constituting the attributes of human personality. The pursued idea was to find the basic elements whose combination would allow a description of any type of personality present in all human groups, or at least in most of them. And this research led to an interesting description..."

This was not Chloe's area of expertise, and she had trouble understanding what Kristen had in mind.

"I know that from the beginning of the twentieth century, psychology has given rise to numerous theories, enabling some undeniable advances in understanding the psyche. From my non-expert point of view, it seems this has resulted in a succession of models and techniques, which are not necessarily consistent with each other, and are even sometimes contradictory. Yet, when used with competence and pragmatic rationality, these models and techniques often seem to be successful when appropriately applied on a case by cases basis."

"That is one way of looking at it... But it is not the only one..."

"Among the multitude of theories, do you want to speak about one of them because it could be used in our project?"

"Yes... or more exactly, no..."

"Uh... Could you be more explicit?" Chloe said laughing openly.

"Well, it's just as I told you..." Kristen said, dragged into Chloe's gaiety.

Then she became serious again, and seemed to change the subject.

"How can one mathematically position a point in space?"

Chloe was a little taken aback.

"By three coordinates, in our usual three-dimensional space (the two dimensions of a map or plan, plus the height)... and if the considered space is... let's say 'a mathematician vector space...' of larger size, then defining a point or a vector takes the same number of coordinates as there are dimensions in this space. But I do not see the connection..."

"I'm coming to it... Researchers have tried to determine if there were a defined number of basic personality traits, such that all personalities can be described as a combination of different proportions of each of these basic traits. In other words, the number of basic traits would be relatively few, but the diversity of personalities would result from the variety of proportions of each of them in each individual."

"In mathematics, this would be called searching a basis in a given space. This involves finding a set of 'basis vectors' such that all the other vectors can be expressed as a combination in greater or lesser proportion of each of these basis vectors."

"That's it. And just the same as in the search for a mathematical basis, the basis we are looking for, in the 'space of personalities', must have two essential characteristics. On the one hand, it has to be 'complete', which means that it is capable of expressing all the elements of the space. In our case it must be able to express all the personalities which we may have to deal with. On the other hand, it must be non-redundant, which means it must have the minimum number of basic features (not more than the minimum) necessary for the description of any encountered personality."

"And did they manage to find the basic personality traits?"

"Yes and no..."

"Another radically committed answer?" Chloe joked.

"Wait, you'll understand why..." Kristen replied, smiling.

"They probably did not find a basis in the rigorous mathematical sense, but they found something that seems to come close; yet, there is still a lot of discussion about the completeness and non-redundancy of the system."

"But how do they know that it works?"

"Now it's time to clarify my somewhat 'ambiguous' answer on whether this is just an additional new theory.

Instead of proceeding as usual, i.e. postulating a theory and checking the cases in which it works, the researchers took a radically different approach, empirical and descriptive, without any explanatory connotation."

"What do you mean?"

"Researchers got the idea that if these independent basic traits exist, we should find traces of them in languages when describing the behavior of individuals. They therefore proceeded by lexical analysis. Among others, but not only, they analyzed all the adjectives in languages which describe trends and behavior of individuals, and tried to group them by family. By means of advanced statistical analysis, they investigated whether it was possible to find distributions of adjectives around some key characteristics that may constitute these basic traits. This research developed over six decades in the last century, with ups, downs and standstills."

"And did they find something?"

"Many say yes... Others are less convinced. Still, all the various independently conducted studies converged on the identification of five factors. These five factors appeared fairly recurrent and stable, looked independent of each other, and seemed to have the required characteristics. And this was in all European languages studied, with the exception of only minor cultural changes."

"And yourself? Are you convinced?"

"Yes... or rather..."

"No?"

Kristen with a smile ignored Chloe's mocking reply.

"Yes... Or rather, partially..."

"And can it be used for our project?"

This time Kristen's response was clear.

"Yes," she said simply. "And besides, it is not necessary for us to be totally convinced by this description, for it to still be useful to us..."

59 - CODE OF CONDUCT

After a little more than one hour, the square began to fill with people. Among those gathering, there were many men with ties and lots of women with stilettos. Small groups had formed, in which the discussions were rife. Sometimes, the tone rose, and the group dispersed. We saw Osc-R and Agn-S, along with Soph-E, heading toward us.

"You were not at the meeting?" they asked as they sat at our table.

"No," Laur-N replied a little surprised, "we had an appointment with you, right here…"

"Yes we had," said Soph-E, "but when I arrived, a couple told me that you would not come because you would be at the meeting."

"And the same thing happened to us; not seeing anyone, we went to the meeting," Osc-R added.

"Nice try of self-fulfilling prophecy on the part of our fashionistas," whispered Laur-N, half-amused, half-annoyed.

"So, what happened at the meeting?" I asked.

Soph-E replied.

"Well, we had a few incantations and duets between Lui-G and the assembly. He explained the will of AG, the Architect Grandiose, recalling that he, Lui-G, was his Mediator Nominated, alias MN. He also explained that he was responsible for transmitting His will. Then it took another twist…"

She paused, and seemed to plunge into a deep reflection. Agn-S continued.

"It appears that Lui-G and his supporters intend to become more, well… directive…"

"What do you mean?" asked Laur-N.

"Apparently, the acceptance of the will of AG, the Architect

Grandiose, must be conspicuous to all, and at any time. For this, Lui-G said, it is important to adopt the recommended dress code: ties for men, stilettos for women. Furthermore, now it becomes necessary to attend educational meetings that will take place every other day at a fixed time. During these meetings it is strongly recommended not to walk in the street, neither drink nor stroll on terraces and not to hold separate group meetings".

"And everybody agrees to comply with this?" I asked.

After some reflection, Osc-R answered.

"Of course, there are those who are already convinced and try to convince others. They are easily recognizable through their dress and their speech. Among the others, their reactions are mixed. Some are seemingly seduced by an explanation concerning their fundamental questions. They are swayed by the convivial atmosphere and the feeling of belonging provided by Lui-G's community. Others seem to be violently opposed to this set of rules; and many seem to be indifferent and not concerned... Lui-G supporters are still a minority, but it is clear that they want to convert some of those who have not yet made up their minds, and they will rely on the indifference of the others to meet their ambitions..."

We remained silent for a while, contemplating the square and terraces, where tense discussions seemed to occur. Men with ties and women with stilettos circulated, looking a little like on patrol. Suddenly, as if she had just remembered something, Laur-N led Soph-E to the fountain. From a distance we saw Soph-E put her hands on her neck. Jessi-K carefully examined her neck and looked at the fountain's statue. Then they came back to our table.

"We have found the missing necklace; the one that matches the pattern in third position on the sphere of the fountain." Laur-N said.

Then again glancing around the square, she murmured.

"All this becomes more and more oppressive. It would be really unpleasant to see this place start to look like a huge cloister, even though it does not seem that there are any physical borders. So what do we do?"

60 - OCEAN

Kristen pursued her explanation;

"A broad consensus has emerged around five factors (also known as traits, or axes) constituting a basis of personality space. The literature refers to them as the 'Big Five'. The first letter of each of the five form the acronym OCEAN, which makes it convenient to remember.

These are *Openness to experience, Conscientiousness, Extraversion, Agreeableness, Neuroticism.*

"Could you explain?"

"Each trait is broken down into 'facets' of its own. The list of these 'facets' will give you an idea of what each feature describes. The terminology of the facets varies somewhat depending on the source, but it roughly gives the following description:

- *Openness to experience*: receptivity to ideas, values, actions, feelings, aesthetics, and fantasy.

- *Conscientiousness*: respect for duty, competence, order, discipline, search for achievement, and deliberation.

- *Extraversion*: assertiveness, activity, gregariousness, search for stimulation, friendliness, and positive emotions."

"Are there always six facets for each trait?"

"Yes, it is a choice, (and besides, the facets of a given trait sometimes can be somewhat redundant). Finally, to end the list we have two remaining traits:

- *Agreeableness*: trust, straightforwardness, altruism, modesty, kindness, and compliance.

- *Neuroticism*: anxiety, hostility, social shyness, depression, impulsiveness, and vulnerability."

"So there are five main features, each having six facets that describe all personalities. How does one scale and quantify all of this?"

"There are several methods consisting of questionnaires, and their outcomes show that these various methods give results which are consistent among each other. For example, one of these methods consists in answering yes or no to eight statements about each facet. Affirmations like:

'*I have a great intellectual curiosity*', or, '*I prefer to work with people rather than being in competition*', or '*I am a tidy person*' etc. Depending on the answer, each question adds points (or not) to the overall score of the considered facet. Hence, for each facet the score varies between the minimum score zero, and the maximum score eight."

"Actually, it's self-evaluation..."

"Research has shown that if the tests are done seriously by self-assessment, or if they are performed by people close to the person studied, the results for the individual's personality are consistent."

"There are eight questions per facet, and from what you say, six facets for each of the five traits (or Big Five), $8 \times 6 \times 5$, that makes 240 questions... I have trouble believing that different human personalities can be identified in just 240 categories."

As soon as she had uttered these words, she put her hand on her forehead, realizing to Kristen's amusement, what she had just said.

"I think that the system thus created, offers slightly more possibilities than 240 profiles," said Kristen laughing.

Chloe calculated.

"Indeed, there are nine possible scores for the first facet (0 to 8). If we now consider the next facet, for each of the scores of the first facet there are nine possible scores for the second facet. So, this makes 9 times 9 or 81 possibilities of combined scores for two facets only and so on. The number of possibilities is multiplied by 9 every time we consider a new facet. Hence, the entire thirty facet questionnaire can generate 30 times 9 multiplied by itself (i.e. 9 to the power 30) different profiles... It's an astronomical number... which is about a billion of billions times the human population..."

Kristen completed.

As you can see, attributing a different profile to each human would only use a fraction of the number of profiles that can be described by such a system. And even if one is only interested in the different combinations of possible scores for the five main traits (regardless of the nuances introduced by the facets on each trait), there are still nearly three hundred million possibilities!"

"Okay, and what is the connection with our project?"

"Well, as you said it yourself, if we want to make a human group behavior simulator, we cannot be content to have agents who are only logical. We also need to provide each of them with a personality profile. Once they get a profile, each agent will enrich and diversify its 'emotional world', according to his or her interactions with other agents and by queries to the knowledge extraction system this will have triggered. I propose to use the '*Big Five*' model in order to equip our agents with the necessary trends, as well as to create their personality profiles."

"And who will answer the questionnaires for creating the profiles?"

"We could introduce our own responses to the questionnaire, as well as those of our colleagues, but it would take time and would not be sufficient if the number of agents we create becomes too large."

Chloe had understood.

"Indeed, it will be easier to invent computer generated profiles, by generating a multitude of random responses to the 'Big Five' questionnaires, according to selected distributions."

Then she paused and murmured.

"It would still be interesting to insert some real profiles…"

61 - HANDSHAKE

As usual, Matthew nimbly climbed up the three flights of stairs that led to Aloïs' door. Long ago, he had concluded once and for all, that there was a glaring inconsistency with elevators… Does it make sense to waste time waiting for an elevator, which one can do without, while one has to spend additional precious time in a gym exercising in order to stay fit?

Aloïs did not seem surprised, and greeted him warmly, almost as if he had been expecting his visit; he had probably heard him climb the stairs.

Matthew never talked to Aloïs about his work for he did not want to bother him with his daily problems. Furthermore, Matthew much preferred talking to him about less mundane subjects, thus benefitting from his distanced vision of the world. But gradually as the project progressed, an indescribable embarrassment had sparked in him, and this time he decided to make an exception.

While preparing tea, Matthew formulated his question.

"In your view, is a system for predicting human behavior conceivable?"

Aloïs did not take long to reply.

"Everything can be conceived… But achieving is another story…"

He paused and resumed

"Basically, this is what economists have been seeking for centuries. Economic behavior is fundamentally human behavior. Indeed general economic trends result from the addition of a multitude of individual micro-economic behavior which take into account, amongst other things, environmental, legal, political, and social contexts. Economists have been trying for a long time to adapt the methods which were so successful in physics to economics; and so they try to formulate all of this into equations."

"I don't feel it has really worked." said Matthew, "If they had found a way to do this, then economies could be piloted the same way spacecrafts are controlled, and judging by the experts' forecasts and conflicting results, this doesn't seem to be the case…"

"Not really indeed…" Aloïs replied thoughtfully.

"For individuals (elementary constituents of human groups), we have not found an equivalent to the equations governing the behavior of elementary constituents in a physical grouping such as for instance, gas molecules or atoms in a crystal."

"No, we have not found… And this is fortunate, because if this were the case, it would mean that each individual is a virtually preprogrammed deterministic being."

"And thus, if it were so, the fate of each individual would be written from birth…" Matthew hinted.

"Not necessarily… and, even in such a case, probably not…"

"Why not?"

"A multitude of deterministic entities interacting with each other, and with individual behavior modeled by known equations, would in reality probably not allow for the predicting individual destinies."

"It's rather theoretical indeed, but I don't see what would prevent one from calculating the movement of each individual over time, and thus being able to predict the position of each element of the system at any time in the future."

Aloïs seemed to gather his thoughts.

"Take a very simplified model. Imagine a game; the 'Handshake Game', consisting of a society of beings who have only three possible activities:

- to be still until someone shakes their hand,

- to move straight ahead at a constant speed,

- and thirdly, when one of them passes close to another, the two shake hands. Each one rotates by a certain angle, and everyone continues in a straight line until the next encounter. The angle at which they rotate is proportional to their distance from one another when they shake hands.

For example, if in order to shake hands, they each have to completely extend their arm, then they will rotate 90°. If they have to half extend their arm, they will only rotate 45° and so on."

"So if they meet face to face, they do not pivot…"

"Let's say that in this specific case, after shaking hands each reverses his direction by rotating 180°. Let me add that they are in a vast enclosure and that when they encounter the enclosure wall, they also rotate by, say, 30° degrees, and continue their way."

"Weird life…" Matthew muttered.

"Not very interesting indeed… The angle values we have assigned are not really important; what matters is the principle of the game.

Let's add that each of these beings is thin relative to the field dimensions, but that they are very numerous; it looks like a crowd… At the beginning of the game, most beings are motionless in one half of the field; and a small minority, placed at the other end of the field, faces them. The 'Game Master' shakes hands with members forming the small minority, and each of them heads straight towards the majority, much like the first shot in a pool game when the white cue ball meets the stationary balls."

"In principle the game should quickly come to life…"

"Yes because, given there is a crowd at the other end of the field, it is extremely likely that there will be encounters leading to handshakes which will put more and more elements in motion, themselves generating other handshakes and movements… and if you wait long enough, the system should take on the appearance of a crowd of individuals pervading all over the field and moving according to encounters."

Matthew did not really see the point of this game, nor what Aloïs was getting at. As if reading his thoughts, Aloïs continued.

"The game in itself is not very interesting… But because the behavior of each individual is completely determined, we can theoretically predict the position of each of them, for example, exactly ten minutes after the start of the game. Another way of looking at it is to say that, if desired, the Game Master can exactly replay a game. The replay will lead to exactly the same situation as in the previous one at the end of an identical period of time, for example, after ten minutes exactly."

"This seems clear to me; in order to replay a game, at the start of the game, the Game Master only needs to put all of the elements exactly in the same initial position, and shake hands in exactly the same way as he had done previously. In such a case the fate of each individual is totally predictable."

"This is where things get complicated…"

62 - ICONS

Gathered together at Osc-R's home, we were looking at our necklaces. We had arranged them on a table with their clasp on the left-hand side.

"I guess that the series of black and white beads evoke a series of binary numbers for you as they do for me." said Osc-R.

Agn-S nodded.

"Indeed, it seems we all have an intimate familiarity with binary numbers. And if black is matched with zero, and white is matched with one, we indeed obtain binary numbers. But one could also take the opposite correspondence, or put the clasp to the right and read the sequence in the opposite way, and then we would get different numbers..."

Laur-N was pensive.

"I think that the black-zero and white-one matching is the right one, and that the reading direction is correct..." she said. But she did not explain further.

"In fact, it looks like a lottery game. Expressed in decimal numbers, I have number 107, Laur-N has 109, Li-O has 77, Agn-S has 100 and Osc-R has 50..." said Soph-E.

"Lui-G has number 70, while our two Invariants have numbers 61 and 47." I added.

"I wonder whether, instead of associating them with their decimal values, we should not look for another correspondence for these binary numbers." suggested Laur-N.

We parted on that suggestion, each of us decided to look on our own.

But soon after, Laur-N joined me and asked me to go with her to the fountain.

"The statue sits on a sphere which has eight patterns of black and white squares, each corresponding to a necklace we have seen. Maybe we will find there a clue to the meaning of it all."

We were walking toward the fountain. The atmosphere was electric and things seemed to take a disturbing turn. Groups of people, men in ties and women in stilettos, roamed the streets. They looked more like patrols than passers-by, and they stared with hostility at those who were not dressed like them. Crossing them, most of the passers-by lowered their heads and hurried along.

At first, we held their gaze, but invariably it triggered harsh remarks, followed by pressing questions about why we did not show our loyalty to the rules of the Architect Grandiose. Since we wanted to reach our goal as quickly as possible, we finally adopted the unassuming attitude of the other passers-by.

Arriving at the fountain, we leaned on the circular rim where the words '*Thank you for responding to this invitation*' were written, and we gazed at the statue.

"I guess she is about to write something on her tablet with the stylus," I whispered, looking at the statue and then at the series of black and white tiles on the sphere.

"Yes, and maybe each tile series corresponds to a letter."

No sooner had she finished her sentence than she bit her lip. We looked at each other, and then, as we stared the tile series again, the message became intelligible... but it still remained completely obscure...

During our meditation on the square, the tension had risen even more in the direction we had come from. There were no longer any men or women without ties or heels, and we were hesitant to go back. We saw the Invariant couple quickly leaving the square. They were moving toward the parking lot where we had initially disembarked upon our arrival in the city.

To avoid the risk of turning back, I proposed to Laur-N to go to the tower since the Invariants were not there. The closer we got to the hill, the less people we met. We began to climb the seemingly deserted path and nobody seemed to follow us. Once at the top, we skirted the tower and after a last look around, I typed the letters S, U, C, H on the digicode. To our relief, the code had not been changed, and the door opened. The slight humming of the fan could still be heard, and nothing seemed to have changed in the room, except the position of the glasses which, instead of being carelessly laid on the desk as previously, were stored in a small casing built into the desk. The wire of each pair of glasses was connected to a small plug inside the casing. We each put on a pair of glasses, but nothing happened until Laur-N had the idea to press the button on the joystick. A multitude of small thumbnail pictures appeared to our eyes, and when we turned our head to one side or the other, we could see them scrolling and new ones emerge. Both of us had access to a pointer that could be moved with his or her joystick. With the pointer I choose one of the first picture of a young man and a young woman, sitting and talking on either side of a desk; I pressed the joystick button. The image expanded, filled my whole visual field, and became animated. Both people spoke about bees, ants and wasps. I selected another thumbnail picture, and this time in another office, the same man was with an individual, a little fat and slightly graying. They were leaning over the loudspeaker of a telephone and discussed knowledge extraction with somebody else.

I took off my glasses, and asked Laur-N what she had seen. She did the same and answered.

"I first saw an old man sitting in a chair, speaking with a younger man about DVDs and eight bead necklaces, and then in another sequence, I saw the same two people talking about sugar cubes, concrete blocks, and isomorphisms."

"What's strange," she added, "is that all of these scenes appear to happen inside rooms, like in offices. There are no outdoor scenes."

"I think that in order to find out what it all means, we should take some time to watch all of these scenes in the order they appear."

"Are we talking about *taking* time or *having* time to study it all without the fear of being disturbed by the pair of Invariants?" she asked a little worried.

Night fell, the lights of the city began to flash, and the hum of the fan grew louder, as if its activity increased.

"It's true, with this interesting discovery I had somewhat forgotten about them, and they may decide to come back... Last time they came here at dusk; so probably we'd better leave quickly."

We put back the glasses in their casing; we headed for the door and opened it; and as we crossed the threshold, we found ourselves face to face with the couple of Invariants..."

63 - BUTTERFLIES

Matthew began to serve tea and, in so doing, he hit the computer table and knocked the mouse on its pad. The small moving computers of the screen saver appeared, and simultaneously the webcam light came on.

"Do you too have this bug with your webcam? It seems to be quite widespread…"

"Yes, it starts on its own, but I don't find it very annoying…"

"Why do you say it is complicated to replay exactly the same game in the 'Handshake Game'?"

"You said it yourself, we need to put all the elements in exactly the same starting position and restart the game in exactly the same conditions. Suppose there is a tiny error. For example, in the orientation of one element, let's say an element of the minority that triggers the game. As the distance to be run is long compared to the thinness of the individuals, there is every chance that this element, which moves in a straight line, misses his vis-à-vis and does not shake the same hand as in the previous game. As a result, he will shake the hand of an individual who is not the same as in the previous game, which will himself begin to move and shake hands with a different element again, and so on… And even if the first one shakes hands with the same first vis-à-vis, if the initial orientation is slightly different, then the distance at which they will cross is different and therefore the rotation angle will subsequently be different too. This will affect the future encounters, and the 'error' will spread and amplify quickly. Eventually, even with only a tiny little difference at the beginning, very soon the actual position of the elements in the second game will no longer have anything to do with what happened in the first game."

"It's called the '*system sensitivity to initial conditions*', I think" said Matthew.

"Yes, and therefore some systems, despite their deterministic components are not necessarily predictable if one does not know their starting conditions with infinite precision. To use a hackneyed phrase, this is what the media call *'The butterfly effect'*.

But back to your original question about predicting human behavior, it is likely that even if individual human behavior was perfectly determined, group behavior would not necessarily be perfectly predictable, because of the uncertainties and small disturbances produced (or not) by their environment."

"All the more so with living beings in general, and humans in particular, where each individual is already itself an ordered assembly of fairly complicated molecules. It will probably never be possible to translate the behavior of individuals into equations the same way one translates the behavior of some molecules into equations."

"That's what I think. One can thus understand why economists and sociologists have so much trouble modeling our societies. They try to figure out global behavior, as do physicists with gas, but it does not work that well. This is because not only are there uncertainties and disturbances, but also because, unlike molecules, human individual behaviors differ one from another, and appear not to be deterministic or fit for being translated into equations."

"In summary," said Matthew, "it will never be possible to create a system that predicts human behavior, be it individually or in groups."

"Predict, in the sense that one could create or discover a 'world' in which there would be an isomorphism between humans and the elements of such a 'world', similar to those already discussed, I do not think so. But to anticipate trends… why not?"

"How come?"

"Let us return to our 'Handshake Game'. In general, the different games will have features that are similar and look equivalent."

"What do you mean by equivalent?"

"Well, most games will lead to configurations having similar disorders and their overall appearance will look very similar to one another after a while from a global point of view. These similarities appear even though the individuals of the different games neither followed the same routes nor had same positions.

Let's take a concrete example… Suppose we take a walk in a train station around 6:00 p.m. The hubbub we hear is the result of hundreds of conversations, footfalls, noises of suitcases being dragged, etc. If we go back the next day at the same time, there is every chance that a hubbub sounds exactly like that of the day before… Yet, people and their positions in the train station are different. They neither exchange the same words nor drag the same suitcases, but the crowd and the brouhaha appear to be the same, indistinguishable from those of the previous evening…"

Matthew was pacing while reflecting and glanced absently through the window.

Aloïs continued.

"It is thanks to these equivalent configurations, toward which systems with many elements evolve, that we can still accurately forecast the overall behavior of gases for example, although these are made of elements whose unpredictable wanderings are very similar to those of the individuals of the 'Handshake Game'. In the case of our 'Handshake Game', we can predict for example that all games lead, after a while, to a distribution of individuals all over the field. Physicists call this the increase of entropy… Physics eventually predicts behaviors of systems composed of a gigantic number of elements, with very high precision."

"OK, but this could not apply to complex beings, all of them different…"

"Human groups are sets made of more complex elements, whose number can be great, but this number is incomparably smaller than the number of gas molecules in a bottle for example. In addition, each element is different from all the others, which does not seem to be the case in purely physical systems. Yet, what is particularly astounding is that we can also predict average human behavior… albeit with a much lower accuracy than with physical systems, but which still remains absolutely amazing… Hence, with a well chosen sample of a thousand people, the opinion of a whole nation on a topic can be estimated with reasonable accuracy."

"This raises the question of free will and freedom of decision…" Matthew muttered.

Besides all his interest in the Aloïs' reflections, Matthew was trying to assess the consequences for his project of what he was hearing.

Through the window a scene caught his attention. He suddenly felt oppressed, and thought he was dreaming… an absurd dream, like most dreams…

64 - REVELATIONS

We were face to face, and the couple looked at us, showing no surprise or emotion. For a moment, no one moved; their presence prevented our exit, and we were impeding their entrance.

The situation was becoming embarrassing. In order to break the silence, I tried a simple "Good evening..."

"Good evening Sir, the man replied."

"Good evening, Madam the woman said."

They took two steps back to let us cross the threshold, greeting us with a small nod when we passed by. Then they entered the tower, and gently closed the door.

We remained silent and surprised, and as we got near the bench overlooking the city, we decided to sit for a moment and once again contemplate the incessant ballet of lights. I felt overwhelmed with new sensations, or rather with a continuous rain of new sensations and feelings that came over me, which, for a brief moment, were giving me an impression of novelty, and the next moment seemed to have always been part of me; a little like raindrops on a lake, which are new only at the moment they touch the surface, and are part of the lake from the next instant.

"I think my name is Leo... I said to Laur-N.

"And I know that my name is Lauren," she replied.

After a while she added.

"I also think the names of our friends are Agnes, Oscar and Sophie..."

"And our famous Mediator Nominated is named Luigi..." I said.

It was warm, and we were feeling good... I watched Lauren; it seemed that without her, everything was less fine... I moved closer to her; she smiled and leaned gently against my shoulder. Then we began to go down the path that led to the city... her hand in mine.

"I believe that we have nothing to fear from the couple of Invariants," I thought aloud.

"Indeed, whether there are one or more identical pairs, they seem not to care about what we do; and I feel that the same goes for the waiters and drivers that we have encountered."

We came out on the street leading to the square, now almost deserted. Further ahead, a woman was walking quickly, with her head down. We saw two men approaching her who seemed to heckle her and, moved by a presentiment, we hastened our pace. Everything happened very quickly; both men jostled her, then one of them, pulling her by the arm, made her fall; and when she was on the ground, the other gave her a violent kick. We had started to run toward her, and again, in a flash I had the impression that a new feeling had come over me, but soon remained only a sensation of disgust and revolt towards the aggressors. As we approached, the two men with ties left after a last group of insults towards the woman. We helped her to stand; she was bruised, but she could walk.

She explained that earlier in the day, she had crossed the two men, accompanied by two women in high heels, and they had ordered her to wear stilettos, which she refused to do. After having comforted her, we walked her home. Then we decided to go and take stock with our friends.

Oscar was at home, together with Agnes. Earlier, Sophie had come, worried. It was increasingly difficult, particularly for a woman to travel alone in the streets without being harassed about her attire. She did not feel comfortable in her home and wanted to be closer to the caring warmth of the small group that we formed. She had asked to be hosted with us. Agnes had offered to leave her apartment and live with Oscar, which appeared to be far from displeasing for either of them. They seemed happy, and I was thinking that the more the atmosphere lightened inside each of us, the more the atmosphere was becoming oppressive outside.

After Sophie joined us, we explained our findings.

"Finally," said Agnes, "things are getting simpler. Since the Invariants seem to have no objection to your visits to the tower, it would be best to return there as quickly as possible, and visualize all the scenes that you can access without worrying about them."

"Things get simpler regarding the Invariants, but get harder regarding Luigi's henchmen..." Sophie murmured. Then she added, as if reluctantly.

"Perhaps, after all, we'd better adopt their dress code in order to go unnoticed and be left in peace."

We reflected a moment on this suggestion, and again, the fleeting impression of experiencing an unfamiliar feeling ran through me, leaving a sensation of rage in me.

"No, it does not suit me. If we do not resist now, we risk getting sucked in something dangerous that will be increasingly difficult to counteract."

"I agree with you... Leo," said Sophie, "in my heart I was not thrilled with my own suggestion indeed."

The others nodded, and I concluded.

"We will go to the tower, and we will be careful, but we will not be disguised!"

We parted, and when back home, I started a small inspection. In my closet, on a small hanger towards the left rear, in the dark, there were two ties which I had not noticed earlier... I knocked on Lauren's door and, when I came in, I started to say, "I looked in my closet..."

"Yes," she interrupted, "me too, and there is a pair of high heel shoes which I had not spotted before..."

Then I added gently, "Since we do not intend to use this gear, ties and shoes can stay where they are... even if we decide to release one of the apartments..."

"Yes," she said with a smile, "in case we would have to accommodate someone..."

65 - COINCIDENCE

Through the window, Matthew intensely watched a black Peugeot which was parallel parking just down the street. It looked like a car he knew. Incredulous, he saw a familiar figure get out. At first, he thought it was a coincidence, but when he saw the figure heading towards Aloïs' building door, he knew it was not the case.

"No, I do not really believe…" Aloïs was saying.

"Not really believe what?" asked Matthew, lost in thought.

"Well, if a sample of one thousand people allows one to estimate a whole nation's opinion on a subject, it is not because our free will is reduced in any way, but it is because the sample was chosen correctly. And consequently, it leads to a good estimate of the general opinion… But what is happening to you?"

"I do not know whether something is happening to me", Matthew muttered, "but I think we'll soon find out…"

They heard the elevator stop, and the doorbell rang. Matthew opened the door and found himself face to face with the Boss. The latter smiled, and as he entered the room where Aloïs was, he greeted him with a warm "Hello Mr. Goebius; how are you ?"

" Ah! It's you… Well, not too bad, considering my age… In fact, much like in home cooking, aging well is the art of getting the most from leftovers!" Aloïs said.

Matthew could not help asking.

"Do you know each other?"

"As you can see, you're not alone seeing enlightened minds," said the Boss cheerfully.

"I don't know whether I am an enlightened man but I can tell you that, even if this is the case still, I can see less and less…"

Despite the light note of the talk, Matthew did feel some uneasiness. While the Boss had no reason to know that he knew Aloïs, the latter knew where Matthew worked. And in this case, each of them had necessarily ended up knowing that Matthew was a common acquaintance. Why did not they say anything to him?

In order to begin to dispel the discomfort that could be perceived in Matthew's question, Aloïs clarified.

"Yes, we've known each other for quite a few years… "

The Boss continued.

"Perhaps you don't know, but actually Mr. Aloïs Goebius knows our company very well and since a long time, because he was one of its founders. As usual for him, when he was convinced that the survival of the company was assured, he sold his shares and sailed on to new adventures…"

"From this time, I started teaching regularly," Aloïs added.

"And why didn't you tell me anything?" asked Matthew.

Aloïs looked at him.

"Well, a few years after your studies ended, when we met again, you told me where you were working and that things were going rather well for you. I deemed it was not necessary to interfere with your work."

Then Matthew turned to the Boss.

"As for me," the Boss said, "I did not know you knew each other until I came to seek advice from Mr. Goebius. I was looking for an innovative project to stimulate the activity and the turnover of the company. Throughout our discussions, the idea took shape to create a decision tool: a system for simulating group behavior of consumers, employees, voters, or any other group facing a situation or a decision. Thus was born project SUCH: Simulator of Universal Comportments of Humans."

Aloïs intervened with a smile.

"You will note, that I do not agree at all on the name, because such a simulator is not universal in any way. At most it is an '*estimator*'of behaviors, whose results will necessarily include a good dose of inaccuracy. But of course, its advantage is that, in order to study a problem, there can be as many 'estimates' as you like, varying or not the assumptions."

Seeming to ignore his remark, the Boss continued

"At the beginning, the idea was just to develop an innovative product to market it, but upon reflection, I thought it would be better to keep its exclusive use for the company. I thought we might use it to sell our strategic advice to business, political, or even governmental groups."

"Again," whispered Aloïs, "I do not really agree... but after all, I don't have any say in the company's business."

Unfazed, the Boss went on.

"The exact nature of the tool, and consequently the development project, should therefore remain secret as long as possible, not only vis-à-vis the competition, but also during its subsequent use, in order to preserve our advantage."

Matthew was silent, waiting for more.

" But back to you", the Boss continued, "I had mentioned that I had great confidence in a talented young project manager, to whom I intended to entrust the direction of the 'SUCH project', and I was amazed when I heard Mr. Goebius mention your name, and ask whether it was you."

This speech, after all quite flattering, had not entirely dispelled Matthew's unease. He turned to Aloïs.

"May I ask you, whether our long discussions about isomorphisms were motivated by your knowledge of the project I was working on?"

"Yes and no, or rather... no and yes... No because, as we have already discussed it, a simple modelization is usually far from constituting an isomorphism, with all the more reason a tool allowing only 'estimations' is still further from that... And, yes, because an isomorphism is a perfect simulator between the realms where it applies, and your project is a tiny attempt to create a 'simulator'... though very imperfect indeed."

After a pause he added.

" But the real reason for the discussion we had about it, is that the discovery of more or less complete isomorphisms, and their use by mankind for the observation and description of its environment, is a fundamental adventure which I find fascinating and greater than ourselves..."

He paused again and concluded with a smile.

"And furthermore, I like sharing ideas with you..."

66 - QUESTIONNAIRES

Matthew was sleeping poorly, probably because of the stress and challenges of his work. He was having strange dreams related to the project, and the beginning hours of his days were difficult. Apparently he was not the only one because the team leaders, except for Rudy, had confided to him feeling the same way.

Since their 'fluke' meeting at Aloïs' place, he had not seen the Boss. Hence that morning, he was not really surprised when the latter telephoned him. The conversation was brief.

"You are now reaching the end of this project which we all have at heart…"

The sentence sounded more like a statement than a question, which was surprising.

"We must now enter the testing phase, and there is still a lot of work…" he replied.

"Nevertheless, I am convinced that we will soon get to something interesting that will allow us to position ourselves as a cutting-edge consulting firm. And this will significantly influence the activity of our company… In order to examine these consequences, I have organized a seminar at the end of the week with the fifty executives whose roles I regard as essential for the future; and you are invited to attend, as well as the managing members of your team.

"I thought all this was to remain secret."

"We'll talk about our future consulting activities, but for now, we will say nothing about the pioneering tool that we have created. If you intervene, it should only concern the consulting business itself, and you will not present your current work. I count on you to advise your close colleagues who are on the guest list.

Albeit politely worded, it sounded more like a convocation than an invitation. Before hanging up, the Boss added.

"Oh, I was about to forget... The place where we will be spending this weekend is called 'Le Clos De Turinge'. It is a hotel converted from an old abbey, and you will appreciate the excellent food. See you on Friday then."

Matthew remained thoughtful, far from enthusiastic about the conversation he had just had... First he thought this impromptu seminar was premature, to say the least, but what annoyed him the most, was that he would not have his own free time for the weekend. The day before, for the first time, he had finally dared to propose to Chloe an escapade by the seaside during that same weekend, and she had accepted... After a while, he had to face the fact that, obviously, he had to attend the meeting, and he decided to advise his colleagues, starting with Chloe.

At first she was surprised by Matthew's unusually morose voice, but she quickly realized what was bothering him, and she replied half-playful, half-serious.

"Don't worry... Of course, this seminar happens a little too soon, but I do not think we should worry about it. There will have to be another one when our simulator is totally completed..."

Matthew did not know what to answer, and remained silent. She continued cheerfully.

"As for the short trip that you proposed to me, it will be for another time... If the invitation still holds..."

"Yes, it will always hold..." Matthew replied, aware of the implicit statement that his response could evoke.

There was a moment of hesitation.

"Have you received the questionnaire that I sent you by email two days ago?" she asked.

"Yes, two hundred forty questions about my 'Big Five', which I'm supposed to answer. It's a bit long to fill in. You sent it to me to scientifically assess the fact that indeed you have not agreed to go on a trip with a psychopath?"

Chloe laughed openly.

"Indeed, there are two hundred and forty questions, but you only have to honestly answer yes or no to each of them, and it will hardly take more than half an hour. Moreover, if you had read the explanation that I attached, you would have seen that the answers are anonymously received and electronically processed. I sent the questionnaire to all those who work directly or indirectly on our project, asking them for a reply for this evening at the latest."

She paused and added.

"Anyway, regarding my future relationship with a potential psychopath, my decision is already made…"

Matthew's pulse beat a little faster, and he had great difficulty to focus again on the project. But in an effort he replied.

"What will you do with the answers?"

"Well, I thought it would be interesting to introduce them into our simulator in order to add real profiles with those randomly generated by the system."

His conversation with Chloe had left Matthew thoughtful in more ways than one.

Towards the end of the day, a strange idea arose in his mind, which he resolved to discuss with Aloïs. Then, as he was leaving his office he received an email from Alex.

"Subject: Your 'random' binary sequence.

Matthew,

You know as well as I do about the existence of the ASCII code. It was the first standardized system for encoding alphanumeric characters. Each letter of the alphabet corresponds with a fixed binary number. Originally developed in order to allow electronic transmission of the English alphabet's characters, it is the source of most of the current methods for transmitting and manipulating Latin scripts…

Instead of simply converting the binary number suites that you have received into decimal numbers, just look at their meaning in the ASCII code, you will get an amazing surprise. I leave it to you, to experience it yourself…

Cordially,

Alex"

He just had to type the words 'ASCII code' into a search engine to see a table listing the values of alphanumeric characters used in computer transmissions in the binary as well as in the decimal notation.

This did not take him long. The first binary number 01000110, expressed by the number 70 in decimal, corresponded in the ASCII code to the capital letter 'F'... When he had finished and recovered from his astonishment, he muttered to himself "Another reason to see him... and tonight..."

67 - TESTS

When Matthew arrived at Aloïs, he was leaning over a Sudoku grid. According to their well-established ritual, Matthew prepared tea, and then asked point-blank:

"Why have you sent me a message in ASCII code?"

"I have been expecting this question for some time," answered quietly Aloïs.

"The eight binary numbers expressing the decimal numbers 70, 61, 107, 109, 77, 47,100, 50, also corresponds to eight ASCII characters: F, =, k, m, M, /, d, 2. In other words it is the expression of your fetish formula... Newton's formula: '$F = KmM / d2$'.

"I gladly accept the term 'fetish formula'. Are you superstitious?" Aloïs replied, as if to deflect the conversation.

"No, I'm not superstitious, it brings bad luck!"

Matthew was aware of the banality of his reply, but he appreciated its 'undecidable' aspect.

"All rational minds think alike, but each superstitious mind is superstitious in his own way...," replied Aloïs with a smile, parodying a famous introduction, so famous that it has almost become a commonplace.

He continued. "Me neither, of course, I'm not superstitious. Superstitions are comparable to chains which, for reassurance, oddly we would voluntarily attach around our feet. But in fact, they only hamper movements and make life more complicated... Still, you're right to consider that the Newton formula is my fetish formula. It has in common with superstition that *it reassures me...*"

Matthew handed a cup of tea to Aloïs, and the latter did not seem to notice.

"In our world of inverted values, games have become more important than bread. And the futility instigators and promoters are adulated, celebrated, and well paid, while the producers of what is essential to live and grow together are struggling to make ends meet. And this simple formula which is the direct and indirect cause of so much knowledge, reassures me. Through its universality, this formula transcends us, and it reassures me about humans' ability to understand and influence their fate."

Aloïs finally grabbed the cup offered by Matthew, who seized the opportunity to ask his question.

"And why did you send it to me in encrypted form? What was your motivation?"

"I didn't send it to you… It sent itself!"

"I don't understand."

"Actually, me neither! I use the formula as a kind of motto in the footer of my documents. I guess, when I made a copy of the screensaver software to give it to you, I must have made an error and inadvertently integrated the formula into the file that I was copying. I only recently got an idea of what might have happened and I intended to talk to you about it."

"But why did the formula's letters and symbols appear as ASCII code on the moving screens?"

"I don't know! Sometimes what emerges from the involuntary combination of computer instructions gives the impression of being akin to witchcraft…"

Matthew was not very convinced, but he did not insist.

"Finally, all that does not matter." he said.

Curiously, whilst resuming his Sudoku, Aloïs said.

"You never know… Think about the sensitivity of some systems to disturbances and initial conditions as we have talked about… this 'butterfly effect' so dear to the media."

Matthew wondered whether it was through humor or a taste for paradox that Aloïs envisaged that the mere expression of Newton's formula, one of the foundations of determinism in physics, could itself serve as a trigger of a chaotic system.

"And the email regarding lateral thinking and Harvard graduated ants… Was it sent by itself as well?" he asked somewhat sarcastically.

"No, that was a joke in order to try to help your brainstorming." the old man conceded with a smile.

'*It didn't work too badly,*' thought Matthew. Then he spoke about Chloe's idea to introduce real personality profiles in the multi-agent system they had designed. Aloïs, while keeping on scribbling on his grid, questioned.

"And who will be the lucky ones having the honor to lend their real profile to test the tool?"

"For now we will use the profiles of those who participated in the project in one way or another. And if you agree, we can include your own."

He looked up at Matthew with an amused smile.

"The least we can say is that I am not a representative of the working population, and I don't think it's worth it."

But Matthew wanted to pursue his idea.

"Since we introduce the profiles of people who worked on the development of a project, why not start our tests on the multi-agent system by making the agents simulate the realization of a project?"

Aloïs put down his pencil and stared at Matthew as if he figured out the rest.

"And what is the project whose realization you would simulate with this tool?"

And the answer came as he expected it.

"Well, the realization of the project SUCH…"

"To say the least, you are not looking for the easy way! So, on your simulation tool, you want to simulate the very development of this simulation tool? "

Aloïs frowned and seemed to fall into an abyss of reflections. After a long moment, he muttered to himself, 'After all, it's not a real simulator… It is only an estimator… and a complex game cannot be replayed…' Finally, he turned to Matthew.

"And when do you intend to start the testing?"

"We will prepare the data for the end of the week, and begin on Monday."

"This idea to make a system act on itself is really a very interesting one, with multiple implications. Two similar ideas, one in mathematics and one at the birth of the computer sciences revolutionized the foundations of these two realms. One of the protagonists named Alan T…"

He paused, became absorbed again in thought, and finally he continued.

"Listen… I'm not very comfortable with the idea of entering the profiles of people who developed it into the simulator and, and then, simulating the simulator's own development… It is a self-reference…"

"But we live with self-references every day… For example, the human brain studying the human brain, speaking about language, or, as we mentioned earlier, the studying of isomorphisms by means of isomorphisms, (not to mention those envisioning that the universe could be closed and therefore be 'submerged in itself')…"

"We need to think and talk together about all this. In the meantime I would like to be sure that you will not carry out these tests before we have discussed them in depth…. But it's late and I'm getting tired. Why don't you come to see me Saturday afternoon to talk further."

Matthew fleetingly thought that decidedly, the whole world was opposed to him taking Chloe to the seaside this weekend.

"Unfortunately, I can't. The Boss has called for a seminar during the entire weekend. We go to 'Le Clos De Turinge' Friday night after work, in order not to 'affect our productivity'… But if that's okay, I can come and see you on Sunday in late afternoon. As I told you, we will load profiles in the simulator and start the tests only on Monday."

Aloïs' face relaxed.

"Okay for late Sunday afternoon… I know 'Le Clos De Turinge'. It is a quiet place and the food is excellent. One of their specialties is called 'Gödel's pretzels'; these are small pastries with strange loop shapes."

Finally he concluded with this odd thought.

"I hope it is a place where one is protected from the wanderings of universal machines…"

68 - PEN

Rudy received the email questionnaire sent by Chloe. He was asked to fill it out, as well as all the team members for which he was responsible. As usual his first reaction was frustration, all the more so since Chloe had remained indifferent to his advances.

With what he had been able to pick up from conversations taking place in the offices, he had also begun to see the project's ramifications. And once again, he was neither the cause, nor even in the secrecy of the decision making process. But upon reflection, he thought that the questionnaire would be a great pretext for getting closer to Chloe again, and try to learn more. Especially since the microphone he had installed in her office did not seem to work and he had decided to replace it.

He waited until the morning of the last day of the response period specified in Chloe's email. He took a notebook and his Montblanc pen, and without prior communication, he knocked at her office door. Though she was careful to keep her distance vis-à-vis Rudy, she received him cordially.

"Some of my team members," he said, "are reluctant to fill out your questionnaire, and have asked what it is intended for."

"You can reassure them. As I mentioned in the leaflet, these questionnaires are processed anonymously and electronically without human intervention. However it is important that the responses are serious and sincere, because they will be used to develop statistical profiles."

"I didn't know that our business also concerned social statistics..." said Rudy, trying to make her talk.

Chloe replied evasively.

"Social, psychological, or other... this is data processing."

She looked at him straight in the eyes.

"In any case, there are not too many people worried, because the list of those who have responded is almost complete. Very few names are missing, which includes yours. If you could send it to me before we leave for the seminar tonight, it would be perfect. I intend to have everything ready today in order to process the answers on Monday morning."

The phone rang; it was Matthew, and Chloe indicated that the conversation would last a while. Rudy left reluctantly, 'forgetting' his notebook and pen in a discreet place, and hoping that Chloe would not notice it right away. He then went back to his office, and decided that, finally, there was no issue for objectively filling out the questionnaire. After all, if his plan worked, next week he would have access to most of what would be said in her office.

The same day Aloïs woke up with a feeling of oppression that did not leave him for the entire day. He felt a dull pain in the chest. It was annoying, but not strong enough to really worry about.

'It must be a beginning of bronchitis. I must talk to my guardian angel nurse, who will visit me tonight,' he thought. Despite this, or perhaps because of it, he plunged into a book entitled '*Alan Turing's Universal Machine*'. Then, at day's end, his discomfort increased. He wanted to call Matthew, but the line was busy. Early in the evening, an immense fatigue invaded him. He walked to his bed and thought, "It's odd, the older you get, the less you want to live, and still the more you are afraid of death…"

69 - MEMORIES

We left early in the morning. We avoided the square and its adjoining streets, which allowed us to reach the hill unimpeded.

"You know… for some time I think I remember…" Lauren said when we were almost at the top.

I thought I knew what she meant, and I had a similar impression. Yet, I wanted to be sure.

"What do you remember?"

"I remember what happened before our first dinner. At first these were fleeting memories, but soon their presence increased, and now I have the feeling that they are part of me."

"I feel the same way." I answered.

She wanted to continue, "I used to work…"

But she stopped, because at the last bend, we saw the two Invariants approaching, probably returning from the tower. When we crossed paths, we greeted them with a nod, to which they responded with an indifferent nod, and we continued on our way.

"I hope they have not changed the code," Lauren whispered as we reached the tower's door.

She pressed the letters S, U, C, H, and as last time the door opened.

We were eager to know whether we could watch all the scenes to which the glasses seemed to give access. Unfortunately, this time the images were frozen, and the dialog box requested 'The Code'. I tried to introduce the letters SUCH, but the dialog box blinked and maintained its request."

After a moment of reflection, Lauren made a suggestion.

"What if we try to introduce the binary numbers present on our necklaces, in the order they appear on the fountain?"

I began to type the first number '01000110', but this gave no result, nor did the other seven binary numbers that I tried.

Then, I proposed to enter the decimal numbers corresponding to binary sequences, and began to type the sequence 70, 61,107... But before I could finish entering all the numbers, the pressing dialog box began to blink again.

It was a great disappointment. We felt that if we did not discover the necessary code, our access to knowledge would be barred.

"First," I grumbled, "why does it request 'THE' code, as if there was *only one* possible code? Is it of universal value?"

As I uttered these words, Lauren looked at me intensely, and we realized we understood each other...

"The message we deciphered on the fountain, seemed to us abstruse... But in fact we know that it is universal..." she said aloud.

"The numbers that we carry on our necklaces, in the same order as that of the fountain, and translated into letters, form a universal code that far exceeds our world..."

So I introduced the eight characters '$F = k\,M\,m\,/\,d\,2$'.

The system unlocked, and we realized that if we both clicked on the same icon, we could both see the same scene.

The door was locked; we could expect to have all the time we needed without being disturbed, except maybe by the couple of Invariants, which did not seem have any repercussion..."

70 - REBOOT

Rudy managed to pass several times by Chloe's office door. Each time he hoped that she would be away long enough for him to act before she locked it and left for the weekend. Rudy's plan was simple: he would enter the office, recover the old microphone which was stuck underneath Chloe's desk, and replace it with the new one. If someone came in, he would say that he just wanted to recover his precious pen and notebook.

As he was beginning to think that he should postpone the operation until the next week, the opportunity he was expecting arose. Chloe left her office and walked to Kristen's. She had just entered into to her computer the profile questionnaires, and these were ready to be loaded into the simulator SUCH.

He entered the room, taking care to leave the door ajar, which he thought indicated that he had nothing to hide in case someone entered.

Chloe's computer screen was still displaying the message 'Ready for loading - Press Enter'. Then the message was substituted by the screen saver. The mini micro was stuck on with a small adhesive patch underneath the table top on the visitor's side.

While he was taking off the defective microphone, someone discreetly knocked at the door, thus startling him; and immediately, the door opened. In the emotion, Rudy dropped the microphone, and quickly straightening up, he got a little tangled in the computer wires meandering under the desk.

"Excuse me," said the confused cleaning lady, "I thought nobody was here."

Then she left, closing the door behind her.

Eventually, everything went as planned. Rudy was able to retrieve the microphone, put on another one and return to his office unhindered…

When Chloe came back, she noticed with irritation that her computer was off. She first tried to switch it on, in vain. Then, realizing that the power cord was not properly inserted into the outlet, she plugged it back into place.

'It must be the cleaning team,' she thought, 'although today, unlike usually, I can't see much difference before and after their cleaning.'

She switched on the computer. But as she was late for the seminar, she did not wait for the end of the restart process. She quickly left her office, and did not notice the message '*Loading Profiles, in progress.*'

71 - PAST

The daylight was fading. Lauren and I had watched almost all of the scenes. In the present one, a dark and curly haired woman was speaking to another young woman; a blonde one.

"So you think that, with the created profiles as well as their logical abilities to ask the right questions and access the knowledge base, they will even be able to reconstruct a past?"

"Yes," replied the blonde woman, "or rather to fabricate the memory of a past; because permanent access to the knowledge base provides them with the necessary notions when they need them."

I interrupted the viewing; we removed our glasses, and I turned to Lauren who whispered.

"Are we only a picture…? A reflection…?"

"It's always an image or a reflection *of something*… What is the image, what is the object? Could it be that this is a matter of perspective? Maybe we just contemplate the border between two worlds forever separated, and which will always remain so, a little like oil and water in the same container."

"Unless these two worlds are inter-penetrable, such as grenadine and water, and the laws governing their evolution forces them to mix," said Lauren without seeming to be convinced.

After a moment of silence, I added, "Finally, perhaps Luigi was not entirely wrong… for the architect."

"Yes, but in this case, it has very little to do with the stories he is trying to sell us…"

She was silent a moment, and then asked.

"Before… before the first dinner… we worked together, didn't we?"

"That's what I think…"

72 - SEMINAR

The atmosphere was friendly at 'Le Clos De Turinge'. After an informal cocktail, the guests settled down for the dinner in a large round vaulted room, made of exposed stone. Matthew was sitting to the right of Chloe. Alex and Kristen were at the other end of the room, and Rudy had just arrived.

… Lying on his bed, now Aloïs had trouble breathing, and a pain was radiating into his left arm. He no longer had the strength to call and ask for help. Suddenly, the pain became unbearable…

"I like to start a meal with a salad," said Matthew, while the waiters began to bring the starters. "This one seems adorned with the famous' Gödel's pretzel' and it looks delicious," Chloe wanted to answer.
But Matthew did not hear the end, or perhaps she did not finish her sentence; he felt as if the lights went out and lost consciousness…

When the lights came back, he remembered that he had a name… something like Math-U… The person on his right offered him some salad… His neighbor to the left believed to be called Chlo-E… At the other end of the room, Ru-D believed he saw a fleeting glow over the heads of two guests; one of them thought her name was Kris-10 and the other believed his was Al-X.

*
*　*

241

POSTFACE

On the front of the Paris City Hall, there is an allegorical statue by Jules Blanchard entitled "Science". It shows a scantily clad beautiful young woman, sitting on a globe which is surrounded with signs of the zodiac constellations. Holding a stylus in her right hand, she seems ready to carve something onto a tablet resting on her left knee.

Perhaps she wants to carve Newton's equation of universal attraction between two bodies:

$$F = k \, (M \times m) \, / \, d^2$$

In order to know the force between two bodies, simply multiply the mass of one by the mass of the other, then multiply the result by a number ... always the same. Finally, divide by the square of the distance separating them; not a little more ... not a little less ... No! You have to take exactly the square of the distance between them. And it works between any object and the earth ... between the moon and the earth ... between earth and sun ... between two planets ... two stars ... two galaxies ... It seems to work everywhere we have tried and everywhere we can measure.

How could a formula of such universality emerge from our primate brains and be so perfectly in harmony with the universe around us? It is one of the first of many such formulas, fabricated by such primate brains, and with a staggering descriptive and predictive character. And these formulas have radically changed our perception of the universe, that of the position we hold therein... and they have also radically changed our daily lives.

Thousands of years have been necessary in order that human brains begin to network and communicate across distances and generations. Thousands of years have been necessary so that these minds, led by some of them with brilliant dazzling obsessions and strokes of genius, gradually build a system of thoughts and languages, enabling mankind to predict the behavior of nature, and start to break free. But the movement has accelerated in an extraordinary way in the last three or four centuries.

Could it be that the system of thoughts, being built over generations, and which seems so well adapted to the description of the universe in which we are immersed, is a sort of decoder in constant evolution? Could it be that this decoder will someday end up revealing the image of the universe, as a DVD decoder reveals the film that is encoded in it? Aloïs Goebius likes to believe it is the case, with his questioning about isomorphisms for which he indulges himself to somewhat stretching the notion. And that wonderful and amazing perspective excites him…

There are some correlations between stories, characters, and certain situations which may, without necessarily representing isomorphisms, evoke them.

The three small mathematical puzzles illustrate in a simple way the power of mathematics as a language and as a way of thinking, but they are not essential for understanding the story. In particular, in the riddle of the halos, two different languages allow reasoning, and both of them reach the right conclusion. However, the one used by Laur-N, which is a mathematical language, is more efficient and compact. In addition, it is more general and can be used for a multitude of different problems.

Most of the problems concerning the description of our universe can only be solved by means of mathematical language, because we do not know any other way leading to predictive descriptions.

But perhaps our exquisite young woman is not about to carve Newton's formula on a stone tablet. Instead of a stone tablet, maybe her tablet is a digital one, on which she contemplates a movie. In which way is the film being played? Forward or backward? If she is watching a movie about the physical universe on a microscopic scale, it does not matter because, contrary to our intuition, physical laws are invariant with respect to time reversal.

But if it is a film about large numbers of particles, or a film in which large numbers of particles interact, then the direction in which it is played is of fundamental importance. The strongly counter-intuitive concepts of chaos and entropy and their relationship to the notion of direction of time's arrow (which itself is on the contrary particularly intuitive and is an inseparable part of our existence) are often misunderstood when encountered. Aloïs Goebius likes to touch on these notions, possibly because he increasingly feels the wounds in his flesh caused by the arrow of time passing... Maybe, it is also to better tame and accept them.

While Matthew wonders about the opposition between "conviction" and "quest for knowledge" for those who use logic (those holding the rope) and about the place of intuition in such a quest, in their world, Li-O, Laur-N and their friends face manipulation, bigotry, autocracy, as well as frontal ensuing oppositions to their quest for knowledge. The high heels and ties, both symbols of belonging, of way of life and of alienation, could evoke (in a non-veiled way) the subduing attempts against young women that some would want to maintain firmly veiled in our world.

"Strange loops" and other "undecidable propositions" invite themselves into this story and in some of its lines (as well as in pretzels), the same way such propositions invite themselves in our world, especially where they are the least expected: in mathematics ... This is a reference to the famous incompleteness theorems of Gödel, popularized with genius by Douglas Hofstadter, but which nevertheless remain really accessible only to a minority of specialists in this part of mathematics. And, speaking about loops, Möbius, whose famous strip inspired so many mathematicians and artists, discreetly associates with Gödel and with this story, through both its structure and its "spooneric" title.

Alan Turing, discovered a computer equivalent to Gödel's work, more accessible to ordinary mortals, by imagining a data processing "universal machine" which can simulate any other data processing machines, and by having such simulation apply to the universal machine itself.
This is what Matthew plans when, despite Aloïs' reluctance, he undertakes to simulate, with the newly created simulator, the project of

creating the simulator itself. And, in the Clos De Turinge, this is probably what makes everything change.

But after all, in her marmoreal calm and far from all these concerns, maybe this beautiful young woman only thinks of the love letter she is about to write to her fiancé. Because, deep down, she knows that, only this is of importance, and only this matters...

TABLE OF CONTENTS